GIRL
VS
BOY BAND

THE
HIGH
NOTE

Also by Harmony Jones

Girl vs. Boy Band: The Right Track

GIRL
VS
BOY BAND

THE HIGH NOTE

HARMONY Jones

BLOOMSBURY
LONDON OXFORD NEW YORK NEW DELHI SYDNEY

With special thanks to Lisa Fiedler

Bloomsbury Publishing, London, Oxford, New York, New Delhi and Sydney

First published in Great Britain in June 2017 by
Bloomsbury Publishing Plc
50 Bedford Square, London WC1B 3DP

First published in the USA in June 2017 by
Bloomsbury Children's Books
1385 Broadway, New York, New York 10018

www.bloomsbury.com

A CIP catalogue record for this book is available from the British Library

ISBN 978 1 4088 7827 9

MIX
Paper from
responsible sources
FSC® C020471

Printed and bound in Great Britain by CPI Group (UK) Ltd, Croydon CR0 4YY

1 3 5 7 9 10 8 6 4 2

To Nancy Zibell, country music fan and lifelong friend

CHAPTER
ONE

Crab soccer!

Seriously? Who came up with that? What evil genius imagined a bunch of middle-school kids "crab-walking" around a gymnasium trying to kick a ridiculously oversize rubber ball? Lark had to wonder: Where was the athleticism (not to mention the dignity) in *that*? It was humiliating! And on the first Monday back to school after Christmas break, no less.

But if she wanted to pass PE, she was going to have to do it, just like everybody else. So she fell into line with the rest of her gym class and waited for the dreaded choosing of the teams to begin. Yet another brilliant gym-class custom designed to torture twelve-year-olds.

Although in this case, being the less-than-stellar athlete that she was might actually work in Lark's favor. If the

PE teacher ran out of those hideous mesh tank tops before Lark got picked for a squad (likely, since shy, lanky girls like her were usually chosen last), she would find herself happily relegated to the bottom bleacher, watching her classmates scuttle around the gym floor like sporty crustaceans.

Confident that she wouldn't be hearing her name called anytime soon, Lark let her mind wander into a song. The possible title was "Everything's Working Out," and the lyrics had been rolling around in her head since the last day of school before Christmas break, when Teddy Reese had been waiting by her locker to walk her to the school bus.

Upside down's turned right side up
The rain's stopped falling, the sun's shining bright

"I choose Lark."

I feel like the whole world's singing along
'Cause everything's working out all right.

The problem was that Lark was suffering from a major bout of writer's block, and she couldn't seem to get any further than these first few lyrics.

Frustrated, she turned her thoughts to Abbey Road. "Wounded Pride," the single Lark had written and the band had released last month, had made a dazzling climb up the charts over the holidays. It was currently at number three! Thanks to Lark's song, social media was exploding with comments about the boys, and their newly launched website was getting more hits than a punching bag. This boded well for the success of their first album, which was due to be released very soon.

"Lark Campbell. Yellow team. Here's your tank top."

Lark felt someone poking her shoulder. She turned to see Jessica Ferris smiling at her. Her first panicked thought was that she'd accidentally been singing out loud.

"Something wrong?" Lark asked.

"Good news," Jessica informed her. "You got picked. *First*."

"Me?" Lark blurted. "Why?"

Jessica laughed. "Maybe it's those long legs. Even in crab mode you're bound to be a good kicker."

"Oh." Lark blinked, shaking the lyrics out of her head in an attempt to focus. "Okay." She took a tentative step forward, then turned back to whisper to Jess. "Um . . . who picked me?"

"That's the bad news," Jess whispered. "Alessandra Drake."

Lark's heart sank. Miss Popular, meanest of the mean girls, and (for today at least) crab soccer team captain, Alessandra stood with her hands on her hips.

"Come on, Lark," Ally said brightly. "You're on my team."

Having no other choice, Lark took the yellow mesh vest

Coach Bricker handed her, then shambled over to where Alessandra waited, her sneakers squeaking on the freshly polished gymnasium floor.

The opposing team captain, Melanie Cooper, looked crestfallen at the sight of Lark joining Ally's squad, but she rallied quickly enough by choosing Brandt Buckley, the best athlete in the entire seventh grade.

After that, the team selection went pretty much as expected. The super-popular kids got chosen early, followed by everybody else. At last Coach Bricker gave an earsplitting blast on his whistle and crab soccer was under way!

In Lark's opinion, wrists and fingers were meant for strumming guitar strings, not for walking on. She decided that if aliens ever attacked earth during a middle-school crab soccer game, they would probably turn their spaceships around and fly away immediately, because, really, who would want to conquer a planet where this sort of madness took place?

As Lark scuttled around the gym, she noticed that Kelly Liu blocked for her whenever she could. And she wasn't even on her team! When one of these blocks resulted in Lark actually scoring a goal, her teammates cheered as loudly as if she'd just won the World Cup. Weirder still, her *opponents* cheered.

Lark was thrilled when Coach Bricker blew his whistle and told them all to "hit the showers."

Luckily, this was only an expression, because the one thing that could possibly be more horrifying than playing crab soccer in gym would be enduring the mildewed locker-room shower stalls *after* playing crab soccer in gym.

Lark quickly changed out of her gym clothes, back into her faded blue jeans and well-worn cowboy boots. Then she pulled her long auburn hair into a messy bun and banged her locker closed, only to find Melanie, Alessandra, and Kelly standing on the other side of it, grinning. The ambush nearly gave Lark a heart attack.

"So what was it like?" Alessandra demanded without preamble.

"What was what like?" Lark asked. "Scoring a goal?"

"No!" Kelly was wrapping a section of her sleek black hair around her thumb. "Spending the holidays with a real live band! Duh!"

"Oh, well, actually—"

"Did they sing carols around the tree?" asked Kelly dreamily.

This earned Kelly a jab to the ribs from Melanie. "Don't be so politically incorrect. Maybe they don't celebrate Christmas," she hissed.

"They're from England," Kelly snapped back. "Everybody in England says 'Happy Christmas' and eats a big old disgusting goose on Christmas Day."

"I think you mean everybody in a Charles Dickens story," Lark muttered, slipping her backpack onto her shoulder. "Anyway, Max and Ollie went back to London for the holidays. I didn't spend Christmas with the boys."

"'The boys.'" Melanie sighed. "It's so cool that you call them that."

Alessandra rolled her eyes. "Well, what else *would* she call them?"

"Lots of things," said Melanie. "The band? The hotties? The rock gods?"

"How about 'the houseguests who finish the potato chips and put the empty bag back in the pantry'?" Lark blurted. "Or 'the guys who rehearse in what used to be my music room until three a.m. on the night before I have a huge math test'?"

The girls stared at her. It wasn't like Lark to blurt, especially in front of A-listers like Ally and her crowd.

"It sounds like you're complaining," said Alessandra, lifting one perfect brow accusingly.

"I'm not complaining, I love the boys—er, I mean, Max and Ollie."

"You *love* them?" Kelly repeated, her voice lifting a full octave, her fingers going into a hair-twirling frenzy. "Like, you *love* love them? Both of them?"

"No!" Lark's cheeks burned and her eyes darted to the locker-room exit. "That's not what I meant."

"Which one do you love?" Melanie asked, ignoring Lark's last statement. "And does he love you back?"

"It's really not like that," Lark assured them. "I don't *love* them, I just love them. You know, as friends. Actually, more like big brothers."

Again Ally, Mel, and Kelly stared.

"That," said Kelly, flipping her hair disdainfully, "is the most depressing thing I've ever heard in my life."

"Seriously," Melanie agreed. "Two gorgeous rock stars living under your roof and you can't even muster up a crush." She wrinkled her nose in a way that had Lark wondering if maybe she *should* have taken a postsoccer shower. "What's wrong with you?"

This had Lark's embarrassment boiling into anger. "Nothing's wrong with me!"

"Maybe she likes someone else," said Alessandra, her eyes glinting like a cobra's. "Maybe someone from *this* country."

Lark did not like being interrogated, and was *not* about to reveal her feelings for a certain adorable, musically gifted eighth grader to Alessandra Drake. "It's one thing to have a crush on a cute musician you see performing onstage, or posing in a magazine," she explained as calmly as she could, "but it's another thing entirely when you share a bathroom with them. Or watch them guzzle a whole can of soda and then try to burp the lyrics to a Rolling Stones song."

"A rolling *who* song?" asked Melanie, looking baffled.

"Max and Ollie are great," said Lark, taking advantage of their confusion to slip between Ally and Mel and head for the door. "But it's hard to be starstruck when you know what brand of zit cream a guy uses."

"Did she say zit cream?" asked Mel, horrified.

"Ewww," said Kelly.

Alessandra was pressing her hands to her ears. "I know you're just saying that to gross us out," she called after Lark. "But I'm not going to let you ruin this for me!"

As the locker-room door swung closed behind her, Lark felt her mouth kicking up into a grin. She finally had a secret weapon for getting Ally Drake off her back: personal hygiene products.

"Today, zit cream," she said, chuckling to herself as she burst out of the gym and into the school's main corridor. "Tomorrow, deodorant! And the day after that—"

"Mouthwash?" This guess came from across the corridor. "Medicated foot powder, maybe?"

Lark stopped short. The voice belonged to none other than that certain adorable, musically gifted eighth grader.

Teddy Reese.

✳

He was wearing jeans and a bulky "Property of Ronald Reagan Middle School Athletic Department" sweatshirt.

Lark found this odd because that morning, when she'd seen him heading into homeroom (not that she'd been waiting in the eighth-grade corridor just to catch a glimpse of him or anything like that) he'd been wearing an Abbey Road T-shirt.

Abbey Road. Once just a classic Beatles album Lark and her father would occasionally listen to between scratchy old records by Patsy Cline and Lyle Lovett, but now one of the driving forces in Lark's life.

Because Abbey Road was the name of the boy band imported from England by the music mogul Donna Campbell (aka Lark's mom). The group had originally consisted of three talented young Londoners, but when one of them was suddenly shipped back to England for "creative differences" (aka really bad behavior), Donna was forced to find a replacement. And in what was perhaps one of the savviest twists in the history of the music industry (okay, maybe not the *entire* industry, but certainly in the history of Donna's label, Lotus Records, which was only one year old), Lark's mother had signed one of Lark's schoolmates to replace the mischievous Brit.

And that schoolmate just happened to be Teddy Reese.

Aka Lark's reason for living.

Okay, maybe not her *entire* reason for living. But definitely her crush.

And there he was. Looking adorable in an oversize sweat-shirt.

"You won't believe what happened," said Teddy, falling into step beside Lark as they mashed their way through the crowded hall.

"Try me," said Lark. "I just scored a goal in crab soccer, so I'm pretty much ready to believe anything."

Teddy laughed. "Well, this morning I was wearing one of those Abbey Road T-shirts your mother had made up as a promotional giveaway."

Lark gave him a curious look. "You were?"

"Yeah," said Teddy. "I was a little embarrassed about it, to be honest. It felt kind of . . . I dunno . . . egotistical or something. But your mom said it would be a great way to publicize the band and I didn't want to disappoint her."

Lark of all people knew how persuasive her mother could be.

"So where's the shirt now?" asked Lark, who was suddenly getting the weird sensation that they were being followed, and not just by kids who happened to be headed to class in the same direction.

"That's the crazy part," said Teddy. "I put it in my locker and went outside to the track. When I got back, the shirt was gone."

"Somebody stole it?"

"Yep. Some sixth grader swiped it, cut it to shreds, then

sold off the pieces for five bucks each because it had, and I quote, 'touched Teddy Reese's rock-god bod'!"

"You're joking!" Lark didn't know whether to be horrified by the crime or impressed by the enterprising sixth grader's marketing skills.

Teddy shook his head. "Coach Evans dug this up for me to wear for the rest of the day, but it's an XXL, so I could probably fit my piano and the rest of the band in here with me. I look like a total goof."

"I think you look amazing," came a voice from behind them.

Lark glanced over her shoulder and saw that this comment had come from a girl in her English class—Chrissy Lawson. They *were* being followed . . . by Chrissy and about twenty-five other starry-eyed girls!

"Teddy would look awesome in anything!" an eighth grader chimed in.

This remark set off a chorus of giggles. The next thing Lark knew, the tall, blond captain of the girls' volleyball team had sidled up and was inviting Teddy to a dance the following weekend.

Lark held her breath, waiting to hear his answer. Teddy had always been popular, and she'd been well aware that she wasn't the only girl in school who'd secretly admired him from afar. But now that he was in a band and on the verge of superstardom, it seemed that "secretly" and "afar" no longer applied.

When Teddy made a polite excuse to the volleyball player—something about a rehearsal with Max and Ollie—the mere mention of the British boys set off an eruption of squeals and shouts. Luckily, the commotion brought Principal Hardy out of her office. When she gave the crowd of girls a stern look, they scattered.

This left Lark and Teddy standing there alone to face the principal's wrath.

But to Lark's shock, Principal Hardy beamed at them. "Lark," she said, "the lyrics you wrote for the band are wonderful. I told your English teacher to give you extra credit for them. And Teddy, when you get a minute, I was hoping you could autograph a photo of Abbey Road for me to send to my niece in San Francisco. She's a big fan."

Teddy smiled awkwardly. "Sure thing, Principal Hardy."

Lark was stunned. Bonus points for writing a pop song? She managed to murmur a thank-you before Principal Hardy disappeared into her office.

"I think that's what's called a perk," said Teddy as they continued on toward class.

"A perk, huh?" Lark gave him a teasing look. "And what are stolen T-shirts called?"

"Occupational hazards."

They continued on their way, laughing together. It was still mind-blowing to Lark that she would be walking this close to Teddy Reese, let alone sharing jokes with him.

"I bet you're beginning to wish you never asked me to play guitar for you in the talent show," she said, remembering the fateful day in the music room when he'd proposed doing a duet in the school talent show. She could hardly believe over two months had passed since, blushing and stammering, she'd explained her extreme stage fright to him. But he'd talked her into it, and in the end, their performance had been a huge success!

"Why would I wish that?" asked Teddy.

"Well, if you and I hadn't performed together, my mother never would have come to the show, and she never would have seen how talented you are, and she never would have hired you to replace Aidan after he got kicked out of Abbey Road. Then you wouldn't have to deal with all this craziness."

Teddy stopped walking and turned to face her. His blue eyes reminded her of twilight in Nashville, and she felt his gaze right down to her toes, which wiggled in her boots.

"A little craziness isn't such a bad trade-off for the awesome opportunity your mom's given me," he said, his tone grateful and sincere. "And besides, if I hadn't begged you to back me up in the show, you and I never would have gotten to know each other, would we?"

Lark felt her cheeks redden; her heart was doing a two-step in her chest. But before she could come up with an appropriate response—something clever, or better yet, flirty, or even just *audible*—the class bell rang.

"Gotta get to class," she squeaked.

And she took off.

✳

After class, Lark found Mimi waiting for her at her locker. Like a Christmas present that had gotten lost in the mail and finally arrived on her doorstep, Mimi was a belated but welcome surprise.

"Meems!"

"Lark!"

The girls clutched each other in a hug. They hadn't seen each other since the day before Christmas Eve. Mimi had been completely booked up with holiday travel and family visits. They had FaceTimed and texted themselves silly, but Lark hadn't realized how much she missed seeing her best friend in person until just this minute.

"Did you have a great Christmas?"

"It was incredible!" cried Mimi. "Fireworks, *posadas*, piñatas, and of course my *bisabuela*'s famous tamales! After midnight mass we had a huge feast at my aunt Josefina's house, and my little cousin Matteo spilled *pozole* all over the shepherd's costume he wore for the nativity play."

Lark laughed. "I only understood about half of that, but I think I got the general gist of it. You had fun, right?"

"Oh yeah!" said Mimi, bobbing her head. "And my brothers and sisters all chipped in and bought me the film-editing software I've been wanting. How about you? How was your first Christmas in California?"

"Nice," said Lark. "Mom surprised me with new hiking boots and a road trip up north to put them to use. We stayed at this really cozy lodge in the woods. No smog, no LA traffic, and—the best part—no cell phone reception!"

"How could no phone reception be the best part of a hiking trip?"

"Because it forced my workaholic mother to leave the music business world behind and just relax," Lark explained with a grin.

What she didn't mention was that no amount of breathtaking mountain scenery could make up for not seeing her father on Christmas. But in true BFF fashion, Mimi was able to read Lark's mind.

"Too bad you couldn't go back to Nashville for a few days," she said softly.

"Wouldn't have been much point," said Lark with a shrug. "Daddy had to work. But he sent me the coolest gift ever from the road."

"New laptop?" Mimi guessed. "Diamond earrings shaped like the state of Tennessee?"

"Nope. A vintage Loretta Lynn album! Rare, and in mint condition!"

"I have no idea who that is," Mimi admitted, checking her dark curls in the magnetic mirror stuck to the inside of

Lark's locker. "But if you like her, then I like her. Same way you like movies directed by Tim Burton, just because you know I think he's a genius!"

"Exactly," said Lark, nudging Mimi away from her reflection, toward the caf-a-gym-a-torium. "Now let's get to lunch. I'm starving."

"You know what would be really great?" Mimi mused as they hurried along. "If one day Tim and Loretta collaborated on a music video."

"It's a cool thought," said Lark, smiling. "But since Loretta Lynn is about the same age as your *bisabuela*, I wouldn't count on it."

"Oh. Well, speaking of music videos . . ." Mimi gave Lark a sly look. "Yours is doing great. But I bet you haven't checked out any of the recent comments."

Lark shook her head. She was still having trouble wrapping her mind around the fact that a few months back, Mimi had made a music video featuring Lark singing one of her original country-pop songs, called "Homesick," and uploaded it on YouTube. To preserve Lark's anonymity, Mimi had posted the song under the name "Songbird"—the nickname Lark's father had given her when she was small and just starting to show her singing talent.

So far, the video for "Homesick" had been extremely well received by viewers—more than eighty thousand of them, according to Mimi (Lark couldn't bring herself to look!). By some miracle, no one at school had stumbled across the video yet. Lark was sure that if anyone had, they would have announced it to the entire student body by now, or worse, identified her by name online. Lark took some comfort in the fact that very few of her schoolmates were into country music, so it was unlikely that they'd find the "Homesick" video while searching the Internet. Still, the thought of being in the public eye—even anonymously—made Lark cringe.

The talent show had been an exception. She'd forced herself to perform because she simply couldn't bring herself to refuse Teddy's request to duet.

"I bet if your mom knew how much attention the 'Homesick' video has been getting," Mimi was saying, "she'd have spent all that time in the mountains trying to talk you into signing with Lotus as a performer and not just a songwriter."

"You're right," said Lark. "My mother knows I hate performing live, and she knows that being in the entertainment industry can be tough on someone my age. But I don't think even that would keep her from trying to make a recording star out of me. I love writing songs for the band to perform, but when it comes to concerts, I'm happy to just watch from the wings."

"Too bad," said Mimi, opening the door to the crowded lunchroom. They moved down the lunch line, and Mimi helped herself to a plate of macaroni and cheese and a butterscotch pudding. "Because you're an amazing performer. In fact, I'll bet my dessert you'll be a star one of these days."

Reaching over, Lark plucked the cup of butterscotch pudding off Mimi's tray. "I'll just take it now, Mimi," she said with a grin. "Because that is NEVER going to happen!"

CHAPTER TWO

Lark put down the guitar and jotted some new words in her songwriting journal. Even though she was struggling to write, her independent study in music was still her favorite part of the day—fifty-five minutes all to herself in Mr. Saunders's music room, with almost-perfect acoustics and an array of instruments waiting on stands and shelves.

Here she wasn't afraid to belt out any lyrics that came to her. Even the silly ones like:

Everything was dark and tragic
Now the world is full of magic
And Teddy's the icing on the cake
How d'you like that, Ally Drake?

As she laughingly sang out the last snarky line, the music room door opened and Lark wished she could gulp back the words.

A face appeared in the doorway.

"Teddy . . . hi."

"Hey, Lark. That melody sounded awesome."

"Thanks. Um, you didn't by any chance hear the lyrics, did you?"

"Kind of," he said. "Were you singing about cake?"

"Yes!" said Lark, flooded with relief. "*Cake.* I was singing about cake. You know, trying to come up with a new spin for a birthday song?"

"Wow, that's a really creative idea," said Teddy.

The fact that he sounded so impressed made Lark wish it were the truth.

Then, as if he'd only just remembered why he was there, he said, "I'm having dinner at your house tonight, so if it's okay with you, I'll take the bus home with you."

"Of course it's okay," she said breezily, her heart fluttering. "What's the occasion?"

"Max and Ollie are back," he reported. "Ollie texted to say they landed about an hour ago. Fitzy is going to make a huge feast, then we're going to rehearse awhile."

A shadow of worry flickered across Teddy's face, which Lark assumed had to do with Mrs. Fitzpatrick's "adventurous" cooking style. The Campbells' housekeeper, affectionately known as Fitzy (because if the kids ever dared to call her Mrs. Fitzpatrick, she'd snap a damp dishtowel at their bottoms!), had a habit of dreaming up peculiar recipes and unexpected taste combinations. Today, for example, Lark had opened her lunch bag to find a tuna fish and banana sandwich.

"Don't worry," said Lark. "If the feast turns out to be hot dogs with hollandaise sauce, we can always order a pizza."

Teddy looked only slightly relieved to hear it; the troubled expression on his face remained as he turned back toward the door. "Good luck with the birthday song," he said.

"The what? Oh, right! Thanks."

"See you on the bus."

✻

The minute Lark and Teddy sat down, girls eagerly began filling the seats around them. An eighth-grade honor student actually got a seventh-grade boy to trade seats with her by offering to do his social studies homework until February.

Teddy kept his head down and tried to ignore the whispers and giggles while he focused on the science book in his lap.

"Are you really studying?" Lark asked softly. "Or are you just trying to keep the fans from fawning all over you?"

"I'm really studying," said Teddy. "I can't get my homework done during study hall anymore because kids are constantly asking me what it's like to be in Abbey Road. And with band rehearsal after school and on weekends, I don't get much time to study at home, either. Not that I'm complaining," he added hastily.

"I totally understand," said Lark. "The band is a huge commitment."

"So is eighth grade," Teddy said with a grin. "I've got a huge science exam coming up, and I'm way behind." As the bus glided past the sports fields, Teddy looked out the window. "And I'm kind of bummed I won't be able to be on the soccer team in the spring," he confided.

"You mean because my mom's planning a concert tour?" asked Lark. Saying it made her heart hurt a little. Abbey Road's first album was scheduled for release in February, right after school break. Donna was already planning a huge launch party, and after that the boys would be going on a three-month tour to promote the record. Missing the boys over Christmas was one thing, but when they went out on tour she wouldn't see them for a really long time.

Teddy sighed heavily. "Yeah. Not that I'd be able to play even if we weren't going on the road. You have to have a B average to try out, and the way my grades are looking right now, I don't think I'd even qualify."

Lark didn't know what to say to that. She knew how much soccer meant to Teddy and she hated the thought of him missing it for either reason.

The bus dropped them off at the end of the long drive that led to the rented mansion Lark called home. She was finally getting used to living like a zillionaire (even if she wasn't really one), though getting used to it and liking it were two different things. As she and Teddy headed across the sprawling lawn, her mind wandered to her old house in Nashville, with its tiny backyard; she wondered what it would be like to sit on the back deck with Teddy while her father fussed over the barbecue and sang old-school country songs.

"There she is!"

Lark blinked out of her daydream to see Max and Ollie sprinting down the driveway to meet her. She'd almost forgotten how terrific-looking they were—one tall and blond, the other dark and muscular. Good thing she'd come to think of them as older brothers, or her knees might have gone weak at the sight of the two boys!

"Go on then, give us a hug," barked Ollie, his blue eyes twinkling as he lifted Lark off her feet and spun her around.

"Enough of that! You'll make her dizzy," Max scolded, playfully shoving his bandmate aside to wrap Lark in a bear hug with his strong, brown arms. "Besides, it's my turn. She's grown about six inches since we've been gone!"

"No I haven't," said Lark, laughing. "In fact, I've positively shriveled up from the pain of missing you!"

"Of course you have," said Ollie easily, looking as though

it were a given that any female deprived of his nearness would have no choice but to wallow in misery.

"Reese!" said Max, releasing Lark to offer Teddy a fist bump. "How are you, mate?"

Ollie greeted Teddy with a bro hug and a few fake punches, which Teddy expertly dodged and returned.

That's what music does, Lark thought, watching Max drop an arm on Teddy's shoulder and lead him toward the house. *It turns strangers into friends.*

Then she let out a yelp of surprise as Ollie scooped her up, slung her over his shoulder like a duffel bag, and jogged up the drive.

She laughed all the way to the door.

✳

The Campbells' Christmas tree was eleven feet tall.

And fake.

That was something they'd never had back in Nashville: an artificial tree. But Lark's mother had reasoned that since they were going to be in the mountains for most of the holiday break, there was no point in bothering with a real one.

When had Christmas become a *bother*? Lark had wondered at the time. Now, as she sank into the living room sofa, she had to admit she was *almost* glad the tree was plastic. If it weren't, she and the band would be gathering around a dried-out skeleton, and after all, the whole point of leaving it up had been so that they could share a bit of belated Christmas spirit with Max and Ollie.

"In England it's bad luck to leave a tree up after Twelfth Night," Max pointed out.

"Don't worry," joked Lark. "This isn't England, this is LA, where the only thing that's considered truly unlucky is when your agent stops returning your calls."

"Or your plastic surgeon," Teddy added, and they all laughed.

"I'm with Max," said Fitzy, appearing with a tray of hot cocoa and cookies, which she placed on the coffee table. "That tree gets taken down first thing tomorrow, or we might as well just leave it up and hang Easter eggs on it come spring!"

As Fitzy flounced out of the room, Teddy reached for one of the mugs, and a red-and-green sprinkled cookie.

"I wouldn't if I were you," said Ollie. "The Fitz was boasting earlier about some new recipe she tried that called for brown sugar . . . and shaved parsnips!"

Teddy looked at Lark. "He's kidding, right?"

When Lark shook her head, Teddy dropped the cookie back onto the plate.

"So what did you do for the holidays?" she asked the boys.

"My family spent Christmas at my grandparents' house," Max reported. "It was beautiful, but freezing. I told them all about LA, and of course, you guys." He paused to shoot a grin at Teddy. "By the way, my little sister, Anna, fancies you, Ted. Wants to know if we'll be touring England anytime soon."

Lark felt her mouth bend into a frown but quickly caught herself. After all, it was ridiculous to be jealous of a girl who lived over five thousand miles away.

"Did you see Aidan at all while you were home?" she asked.

"Only on the telly," said Max.

Lark's eyes went wide. "Aidan's been on TV?" She hoped he wasn't a lead story on the evening news, but knowing what a troublemaker Aidan was, that was entirely possible!

"He's actually making a name for himself on *Sound Off*," Ollie reported. "It's one of those musical talent competition shows."

"Aidan's a solo act now," Max said. "It's perfect for him, since he's too self-centered to be a team player." He laughed. "But the boy does have talent. He's made it through the first round. A lot of people think he might win."

"Aw, who wants to waste time talking Aidan, when we could be giving gifts?" said Ollie, handing Lark a large package with a squashed bow. "This is for you, from Maxie and me. It's from Camden Market."

"That sounds way cooler than 'we got it at the mall,' doesn't it?" said Lark, accepting the gift.

"Sorry it looks a bit shabby," said Max. "Customs and all."

Lark tore into the wrapping paper and opened the dented box to find a pair of flower-print Dr. Martens.

"Thought you might give those old cowboy boots of yours a rest now and then," teased Max. "Do you like 'em?"

"I love them!" cried Lark, slipping her new boots on.

"Very rock 'n' roll," Ollie observed. "Now all you've got to do is dye your hair bright green and you'll be good to go."

Teddy grinned. "Please don't do that."

"I agree," said Max, reaching out to ruffle Lark's long, auburn hair. "It's brilliant just the way it is."

Blushing, Lark reached under the tree and pulled out three envelopes, which she handed to Max, Ollie, and Teddy. "These are from me and my mom," she said as the boys opened them.

"Tickets to opening day at Dodger Stadium," said Ollie. "That's epic. I've always wanted to go to a baseball game."

"Amazing," Max agreed, smiling. "Although I'm surprised Donna hasn't booked us to sing the national anthem while we're there."

"Oh, she's working on that," Lark assured him.

"Here's one for you, mate," said Ollie, tossing a package to Teddy.

"Thanks," said Teddy, ripping open the wrapping and beaming at what he saw inside.

"What is it?" asked Lark.

Teddy held up a red-and-white scarf with a crest emblazoned on it.

"That's the official Arsenal team scarf, Ted!" Max explained. "Thought you'd like it, since you love footie as much as we do."

"It's awesome," said Teddy. "But . . . I feel bad. I don't have anything for you guys."

Ollie let out a loud crack of laughter. "But you've already given us the best gift ever . . . you saved the band! And now you're in it for the long haul, mate! Abbey Road forever!"

Lark noticed that Teddy suddenly looked very uncomfortable.

"Thanks," he said again, putting the scarf around his neck.

"All right then," said Max, gulping the last of his hot cocoa and leaping to his feet like the agile dancer he was. "Time to get to work!"

✳

Lark tried to concentrate on her homework, but the thought of the boys rehearsing in the practice room above the garage had her fingers itching to strum her guitar. Halfway through her science chapter she gave in, picked up her beloved Gibson, and worked on her new song.

She was concentrating so hard she almost didn't hear the knock on her bedroom door. When she looked up, her mother was peeking in, smiling broadly. "The song sounds great. Another hit for Abbey Road?"

"Mother . . ." Lark rolled her eyes.

"Sorry, but I wouldn't be much of a label boss if I didn't at least ask. The boys are already at the dinner table. If we don't hurry, there might not be anything left for us."

"Is that a bad thing?" said Lark, popping off the bed with a smile. "I mean, with Fitzy's cooking, we might be better off."

"I made her promise to keep it simple tonight," said Donna, taking Lark's hand as they headed for the stairs. "No exotic spices, no wacky flavor combinations. Just a plain old roast."

Lark grimaced. "Please tell me you specified what kind of meat she should be roasting. Knowing Fitzy, it might be wild boar. Or rattlesnake."

They found the boys arranged around the kitchen table, and Lark was happy to see that Teddy had seated himself in the chair beside her usual one.

Fitzy, in an apron reading, If at First You Don't Succeed, Fry, Fry Again, was already serving the meal: roast beef, mashed potatoes, and peas, all of which smelled deliciously ordinary.

"Please pass the potatoes," said Lark, slipping into her chair.

As Ollie reached for the bowl, he accidentally brushed his cuff through the gravy on his plate, smearing it with brown sauce.

"Bloody hell," he grumbled. "And I just got this for Christmas."

"Hand it over," said Fitzy, pointing to the shirt. "If I don't pretreat it right away, it'll never come out in the wash."

Obediently, Ollie stripped down to his under-shirt . . . revealing a dramatic tattoo! Black, green, and blue ink stretched from his wrist to his shoulder in the shape of a terrifying, red-eyed dragon.

Lark gasped. Teddy stared.

And Donna went pale. "What in the world . . . ?"

"Did you join a biker gang over Christmas?" Fitzy asked, appalled.

"Tattoos are an art form," said Ollie calmly.

"Not in this house they aren't!" cried Donna. "I thought I was clear about Abbey Road being a clean-cut, wholesome group!"

"You mean you don't like it?" asked Ollie with an expression of wide-eyed innocence.

"Of course she doesn't like it!" said Lark. "Even Aidan dressed head to toe in black leather looked like a choir boy compared to you. Are you crazy?"

"*We* aren't," said Max, biting back a smile. "But you must be if you think a bloke as vain as Ollie would ever do anything to mess with his perfect appearance."

No longer able to keep a straight face, Ollie cracked up. "Nothing to panic about," he said. "It's just one of those temporary deals."

Teddy leaned toward Lark and smiled. "So I guess I shouldn't tell your mom about my upcoming nose-piercing appointment?" he whispered.

Lark giggled. "Not if you value your life," she replied.

"Don't be angry," said Max, his eyes twinkling. "We were just having a laugh, all in good fun."

By now, the color had returned to Donna's face. "So you think giving your manager a heart attack is fun?"

"Just for that," said Fitzy, tucking Ollie's shirt under her arm and heading for the laundry room, "no dessert for either of you! And I even made something special—the perfect British dessert to go with the roast, just in case you were feeling homesick."

"What's that?" asked Max eagerly. "Treacle tart? Banoffee pie?"

"Yorkshire pudding!" she called over her shoulder.

At this, Max and Ollie burst out laughing all over again.

"What now?" asked Lark.

"Oh, nothing," said Max, cracking up. "It's just that Yorkshire pudding isn't usually a dessert at all, it's—"

A scowl from Donna cut him off.

Max finished in a mumble, "Uh, it's delicious, that's what."

"I'll shower right after dinner and get rid of this," Ollie assured Donna. "Sorry to have given you a fright." With an apologetic smile, he handed her the bowl of buttery mashed potatoes.

But Donna waved off his peace offering with a horrified look. "You should know, Oliver, there's only one thing I hate more than tattoos."

"What's that?" asked Ollie.

"Carbohydrates," Donna answered.

✳

After dinner, Donna ordered Ollie to make good on his promise to wash off his tattoo, and then go straight to bed; she advised Max to call it a night as well.

"Big day tomorrow," she told them. "The countdown to the release of your first album begins and that means we've got lots of work to do. Starting with a photo shoot."

Neither boy argued; they were clearly exhausted from their long flight.

"Bet you're glad to have them back," Teddy whispered to Lark.

"Well, they do liven up the place," Lark agreed with a grin. The truth was, it had been much too quiet in the house without them and although she knew she was in for a world of teasing, she couldn't have been happier about their return.

"You should turn in early too, Teddy," said Donna. "I'm sending a car to pick you up at school right after third period. Your parents have cleared it with the principal. I'll have your wardrobe waiting at the photo studio when you arrive."

Teddy looked panicked.

"Mom," said Lark, "I think Teddy has a science test tomorrow."

"Fourth period," Teddy clarified.

Donna gave him a breezy smile. "Well, you'll just have to take a makeup test, won't you?"

With that, she strode out of the foyer toward her office.

Before Lark could say anything else about the science exam, Teddy's father pulled into the drive and honked the car horn.

"Thanks for dinner," Teddy said glumly, and disappeared out the door.

"What, no kiss good night?" teased Ollie after he'd gone.

Lark narrowed her eyes at him. "No, of course not. We're just friends, and besides—" The idea of kissing Teddy sent a tingle up her spine.

"Besides, you wouldn't want me and Maxie witnessing your first snog, right?" Ollie chuckled.

Lark's cheeks turned pink.

"Ah, don't blush," said Max, following a yawning Ollie

up the stairs. "We know you're mad for that boy." When he reached the top step, he turned to give Lark a sleepy grin. "The good news is, it's definitely mutual."

Cheeks flaming, Lark spun on her heel and bolted for the kitchen, wondering if maybe "much too quiet" hadn't been such a bad thing after all!

CHAPTER THREE

"Eighty thousand thirteen," Mimi proclaimed.

"Eighty thousand thirteen?" Lark repeated, flipping the pages of her math book. "Is that the answer to the division problem, or the word problem?"

Mimi giggled. "Neither. It's the answer to: How many likes has 'Homesick' gotten since I posted it on YouTube?" She turned her laptop screen so Lark could see it. Sure enough, there was the enigmatic, mysterious Songbird, floating on a raft in the Campbells' swimming pool, singing happily in the sunshine. "Look at all the comments!" Mimi gushed. "Eight hundred and twelve!"

The number was fairly staggering, Lark had to admit. And a bit nauseating, too. Lark's natural shyness made her want to avoid fame at all costs.

"We're supposed to be studying for our math test," she

said, hoping to shift Mimi's focus. "I know we've been on break for two weeks, but you do remember what studying is, don't you?"

"This *is* studying," Mimi countered. "I'm studying to be a world-renowned filmmaker."

"And what about the ten zillion questions you asked me about Ollie and the band before we started?" Lark teased. "Was that you being a filmmaker, too?"

"No, that was me being a girl with a crush." Mimi grinned, owning it. "And since you've brought him up again . . . I can't believe Ollie got back yesterday and I still haven't laid eyes on that beautiful boy. Hey, do you think he'd let me make a documentary about him?" She furrowed her brow in thought. "I can call it *A Day in the Life of Britain's Most Gorgeous Pop Star*."

Lark laughed, because she knew this documentary, if it ever happened, would just be an excuse for Mimi to follow Ollie around for twenty-four hours straight, her camera ready to capture his every action—from rehearsing his dance steps to trimming his fingernails.

"Even if Ollie *would* let you, you know you'd have to get permission from a higher authority."

"Right. Your mom."

"It's not that it isn't a great idea," Lark added quickly. "But the boys are majorly booked up right now. Poor Teddy. He can't even find time to study."

Mimi let out a long sigh. "Is he dating anyone?"

Lark's heart sank. "Teddy? Dating? Who would he be dating?"

"Not Teddy . . . *Oliver*," Mimi clarified. "Did he mention going on any dates while he was back in London? Maybe he went out with that nasty Jade girl who came between him and Aidan?"

"No, he didn't mention dating Jade or anyone else," Lark assured her gently. She knew that Mimi believed she was in love with Ollie. But she also knew that while Ollie was fond of Mimi, at nearly sixteen he was much too old for her.

Satisfied that Ollie's heart had not been stolen over Christmas, Mimi smiled. "Good. So we can get back to the topic at hand."

"Math?"

"Movies! I've been comparing our work to that of all the other seventh-grade-director-slash-songwriter partnerships out there, and guess what. There aren't any! Which means we're completely original!"

"Or completely crazy," Lark muttered. "Did it ever occur to you that maybe the reason there aren't any other seventh graders making music videos is because they're all too busy doing their homework?"

"Nope. Never occurred to me at all. What *did* occur to me is that we should make another one!"

Lark nearly dropped her textbook. "What?!"

"You're a sensation," Mimi reasoned, undaunted. "The

fans want more. And you have a new song, so what are we waiting for?"

"We're waiting for me to decide if I want to be a performer, that's what," Lark reminded her. "And for the record, I don't see that happening anytime soon."

"But you won't be on a stage," Mimi pointed out, sliding the laptop closer to Lark. "You'll be on the Internet. There's a huge difference."

"Not to me there isn't. Now, can we please get back to our math?"

"Not until you check out the amazing stuff people have been writing about you."

Reluctantly, Lark squinted at the computer screen and began to read the comments:

I LOVE LOVE LOVE this song! Homesick is totes awesome.

SO YOUNG, SO TALENTED, SO COOL! Go Songbird!!!!!!

WHO IS SHE? WHEN IS SHE TOURING?

Some of the comments were just long lists of emoji—clapping hands, hearts, smiley faces, and guitars. One fan even invited Songbird to play at her sweet sixteen birthday party.

"Don't tell me this doesn't make you proud," said Mimi with a grin. "I'd kill for a single comment complimenting the creative camera angles."

"Of course I'm flattered that people like it," Lark conceded, scrolling down through the comments. "But what about the people who don't? Look . . . someone typed in, like, fifteen thumbs-down emoji. And this person calls me 'A NOBUDDY in uglee boots'? And what about this person, GlitzyGirlFluffyFace? She says, 'Put Songbird back in her cage and lock the door, ASAP!'"

Mimi rolled her eyes. "Do you really care what someone who calls herself GlitzyGirlFluffyFace thinks? Please!"

"It's mean."

"Yes, it is," Mimi agreed. "But think about it: of all those eight hundred and twelve comments, you've only found three nasty ones. So that's only . . ." She picked up her smartphone, called up the calculator, and tapped in the numbers. "Point zero zero three six nine percent negative." She quirked an eyebrow at Lark. "You have a less than one percentage of haters. How's *that* for math?"

Lark had to laugh. Mimi was right—GlitzyFluffy-What's-Her-Face was just a mean-spirited stranger and there was no reason to care what she thought, especially since the overwhelming majority of viewers had enjoyed what Lark and Mimi had created.

"But what if it's a fluke?" asked Lark, not realizing how much she hoped it wasn't until she'd actually spoken the words out loud.

"If it is, there's only one way to find out." Mimi shrugged. "If we post a second video and it does as well as or better than 'Homesick,' then it's not a fluke."

"Then what?" Lark asked warily.

"Then you have to tell your mother. About both of them."

Lark frowned. "You drive a hard bargain, Mimi Solis."

"What can I say?" Mimi tossed her hair in an exaggerated gesture of faux arrogance. "I'm a creative genius *and* a shrewd businesswoman!"

※

Lark hadn't brought her guitar along to do her math homework, but Mimi said it wasn't a problem; they could dub in the music later on. For now, Lark would just sing "Everything's Working Out" a cappella.

"Okay, so I'm thinking that we should just have fun with it," Mimi said, in director mode. "The song's about being carefree—so let's try to capture that in your actions, too."

First Lark skateboarded around Mimi's driveway, wobbling and tottering and laughing as she sang the lyrics, "*Life's a crazy ride, but time is on my side . . . I know I'll reach my goal, 'cause that's just how I roll."*

Next, they went to the backyard and Mimi had Lark jump on the trampoline, shooting her from below to give the illusion that Lark was flying—the perfect image for the upbeat mood of the song.

There was a bit of a glitch when Mimi's little sister, Lola, arrived home from school with her two best friends from third grade, Casey and Jane. Lola demanded that Mimi and Lark vacate the backyard immediately so she and her friends could practice cartwheels and handstands.

"We were here first," said Mimi.

"Well, we were here second."

"I'm older."

"I'm younger!"

Lark knew this would get them nowhere, but she'd spent enough time at Mimi's house to understand that this was the kind of ridiculous argument that could only happen between siblings. Mrs. Solis came outside and refereed the shouting match. It was so long and so loud that Mr. Solis, who was working in his home office, threw open the window and provided backup for his wife from the second floor.

Ultimately, the decision went in Mimi's favor, and Lola and her friends were sent next door to practice their cartwheels in Casey's yard, which, as Lola observed snippily, was "way flatter and shadier" than the Solises', making it far better for gymnastics anyway.

Lark witnessed the entire hullabaloo in wonder, and with a twinge of jealousy. Watching Mr. and Mrs. Solis work as a team to keep their daughters from tearing each other's hair out had made her miss the days when her own mother and father had enjoyed a similar kind of partnership.

"I'll make it up to her by filming one of her gymnastics competitions," Mimi told Lark.

Lark smiled. "You're a good big sister."

"But I'm an even better filmmaker! So let's get back to work!"

Under Mimi's direction, Lark hula-hooped, cartwheeled, and climbed a tree, all while singing her new song.

When they were finished, Mimi was thrilled with the footage. "My new software will make it really easy to add the music," she explained. "We'll have to schedule a recording session soon. Check your calendar, and we'll set something up."

Lark smiled. "You sound like a real-life music mogul," she teased, just as her phone sounded in her pocket. The ring tone was the one she'd assigned to incoming calls from her mother: the Garth Brooks hit "Mom."

"Speaking of real-life music moguls . . . ," she said,

laughing as she slid her finger over the answer bar and brought the phone to her ear. "Hey, Mom. What's up?"

Lark listened for less than a second, then let out a shriek of joy. Mimi, who was viewing the video again, nearly jumped out of her skin.

"What was that about?" she asked, when Lark finally ended the call.

"My mom just told me my dad's coming to LA," Lark reported excitedly, "to play backup guitar for the Hatfields this Saturday night. He got us two tickets."

"That's awesome," said Mimi. "Especially since you didn't get to see him for Christmas."

Lark sighed. "It is, except in true Donna Campbell form, my mom's already arranged a business dinner for that night, which she absolutely can't cancel."

"That's too bad," said Mimi.

Lark's eyes sparkled. "Not really. You can come in her place. It'll be our first concert!"

Mimi opened her mouth to respond, but Lark held up her hands. "I know what you're going to say: you have no idea who the Hatfields are, but I promise you'll love them. They're a huge country band. We'll have so much fun! We can even go backstage after the show."

"I'd love that," said Mimi. "But it's my cousin Gabriella's *quinceañera* that night. I've promised to film the whole event, as my birthday gift to her."

"Oh," said Lark. "Well, that sounds awesome, too. Wish Gabriella happy birthday for me."

"I have an idea who you can ask instead," said Mimi, waggling her eyebrows suggestively.

"Forget it," said Lark. "It would be too weird!"

Mimi laughed. "You say weird, I say romantic."

CHAPTER FOUR

On Friday afternoon, Lark stepped off the school bus and groaned. One glance at the line of cars parked in her driveway told her exactly what she was in for. All those Porsches, Escalades, and other luxury vehicles she didn't know the names of could only add up to one thing: Abbey Road's ever-growing team of music-industry professionals had descended upon the Campbells' house.

"Great," she muttered, hoisting her backpack onto her shoulder and making her way up the drive. She really wasn't in the mood to deal with a house full of strangers today—she had an English paper to write and two history chapters to outline. On top of that, she was totally on edge because today was the day Mimi had promised to finish editing the "Everything's Working Out" video and post it.

Lark couldn't decide whether she was hoping for a good

response or a bad one. If the video received less than one hundred thousand likes, Mimi had promised to keep the secret of Songbird's identity from Lark's mother. But if it did as well as Mimi was predicting it would, Lark had promised to tell Donna, and risk being pressured to take her talent public.

But most irritating of all was the fact that Lark still hadn't found anyone to join her at the Hatfields concert. She'd mustered up the nerve to invite her lab partner, Emma DiGiorgio. Emma had been thrilled, and the girls were halfway through planning their postconcert sleepover when Emma suddenly remembered that Saturday was her parents' wedding anniversary and the whole family was going out for a big, fancy dinner.

This stung for two reasons: one, Lark still didn't have someone to go to the concert with, and two, it made her realize that she'd never get to celebrate her parents' wedding anniversary again, since technically they no longer had one.

Depressing.

On the front porch, she let out a long rush of breath, then opened the door to a hurricane of noise and activity.

It was even worse than she'd expected. The foyer was overrun with Donna's employees, all of whom were making plans for either the launch party or the concert tour. There seemed to be an extremely heated difference of opinion regarding the canapes that would be served at the party (mini quiches *out*, salmon mousse puffs *in*) and someone was arguing on the phone with a concert promoter about what sort of bottled water should be awaiting the boys at their performance venue in Tallahassee, Florida.

Lark zigzagged her way through the crowd to the kitchen, only to find more madness. The entire kitchen table was strewn with official-looking documents for the boys to sign, and Lark counted no fewer than four lawyers dressed in sharp suits sifting through the contracts and agreements, heatedly debating various clauses and conditions. The breakfast bar held two laptops. One was playing the unedited cut of the music video the boys had filmed that morning.

Grabbing a snack from the fridge, Lark stopped to watch the footage. She hated to admit it, but she wasn't especially impressed. The song was great and the boys, of course, looked amazing. But she suspected Mimi would call the direction "predictable" and the mood "uninspiring." She wasn't about to mention this to the video director, though, who was probably charging Lark's mother a fortune for his mediocre work.

On the second computer's screen were album-cover graphics, which a guy who didn't look much older than Lark was proudly showing to her mom.

"The colors are terrific," said Donna. "But I don't like the font you've used for the words 'British Invasion.' Can you try using a funkier typeface for the album title?"

At that moment, a flustered PR rep came barreling into the kitchen, smartphone in hand, eyes practically bugging out of her head in alarm. "Donna, did you give Oliver permission to tweet this?"

"Tweet what?" asked Donna. "I didn't give him permission to tweet anything." She whipped her head back to the laptop and pointed to Max's image on the screen. "You've made his eyes much too green!" she scolded the designer. "For God's sake, he's a teenage boy, not a feral cat!"

As the graphic designer began punching computer keys, Donna turned back to the PR rep. "Now, Julia, what's this about a tweet?"

The rep held out the phone so Donna could read the Twitter post for herself. Lark watched as her mother's gaze darted across the screen, her eyes narrowing as she took in the 140 characters.

"Oliver Wesley!" she exploded, in a tone so blood-curdling that it even made the lawyers jump. "You're in big trouble, kiddo!"

Lark couldn't imagine what Ollie had tweeted, but she sure didn't want to be around when he tried to explain himself to Donna. She quickly ducked out of the kitchen and followed the sound of thumping music into the family room, only to find that all the furniture had been pushed to one end of the expansive space and the carpet had been rolled up. In the middle of the floor stood Ollie, Max, Teddy, and Jas, the boys' choreographer.

"From the top," Jas called out over the music—a bouncy dance track from the upcoming album called "Tremble." "Five, six, seven, eight . . ."

They zipped through a series of highly complex and incredibly cool moves. Lark watched in awe as Max made the routine his own, lending his jaunty grace to every step. She was equally impressed by Teddy, and realized with a flutter of her heart that this was only the second time she'd ever seen him dance.

She sincerely hoped it wouldn't be the last.

When the song finished, the boys staggered breathlessly to the sofa and collapsed.

"Nice work, fellas," said Jas. "I like the way you all put your own spin on it. In fact, I think this might be the best routine for you guys to perform at the launch party." He offered each boy a high five. "I'll go grab you some waters."

"Speaking of the party," said Ollie, "I'll ask Donna to invite loads of supermodels."

Lark rolled her eyes. "You love winding my mom up, don't you?"

"It's my specialty," said Ollie, throwing her a wink.

"Are your parents looking forward to the party?" Lark asked Teddy.

Teddy laughed. "Oh yeah. My mom's already stressing out about what to wear."

"Do you think your families will be able to make it from England?" she asked, turning to Ollie and Max.

Ollie shook his head. "Wish they could. But my parents will be on a cruise of the Greek islands."

Lark felt an ache in her heart when she saw the sadness in Max's eyes.

"My family would love to come," he said, dropping his gaze to the floor. "Especially Anna. But the airfares are just too expensive."

Just then, Donna came dashing into the room with Julia, the PR rep who'd ratted Ollie out for his cheeky tweet, on her heels.

"We just got incredible news," Donna gushed. "Julia had a call from the producer of *Rise and Shine*!"

"Is that the morning talk show with the meteorologist who sings his weather reports?" Lark asked warily. "And the tap-dancing traffic girl?"

"That's *Up and At 'Em, LA*," said Teddy.

"*Rise and Shine* is a national show, so it caters to a much larger market," said Donna importantly. "And thanks to Julia's top-notch public relations skills, they've just confirmed an interview with Abbey Road for this coming Tuesday with entertainment reporter Bridget Burlington-Carzinski. She wants to do the broadcast live, right here. It will be an expanded segment—an 'at home with pop music's latest stars' sort of thing."

Lark was immediately reminded of Mimi's fantasy about shooting a "day in the life" documentary about Ollie. Apparently, Mimi really did think like the professionals. One look at Teddy, however, told her he was thinking like a kid with a class schedule.

"What about school?" she asked.

"It's a *morning* show," said Julia haughtily. "The crew will be here to set up by four thirty—"

"In the *morning*?" Max said. "Oi."

Julia ignored him. "You'll start filming at five thirty. The interview will last approximately thirty minutes, which means you'll be done by six."

"You'll have plenty of time to make it to homeroom before the bell," said Donna with a triumphant smile.

"Our first appearance on American television," said Ollie. "Can you believe it, Max?"

Max grinned. "First of many, hopefully."

"Congratulations," Lark told the boys, but at the same time she was making a mental note to have something else to do at dawn on Tuesday.

Something as far away from the TV cameras as possible.

❋

Lark spent the rest of the afternoon in her room, trying to concentrate on her homework, but the noise from downstairs made it nearly impossible. Just before dinner, she heard the sound of car doors in the driveway and peeked out the window to see that the interlopers were finally calling it a day.

Not a moment too soon! She was starving.

Grabbing a folder out of her backpack, she hurried downstairs to find Fitzy placing an order for three large pizzas. Lark's mouth watered thinking about the yummy cheese and crispy pepperoni. She'd just have to be quick enough to snag her slice before the boys devoured them all, or before Fitzy got it in her head to sprinkle the pizza pies with shredded endive or grated ginger root.

"Where are the boys?" she asked her mother, who was hunkered down at the kitchen table, going over the contracts the lawyers had left.

Donna motioned with her head toward the family room. "They're thoroughly exhausted," she said. "Honestly, you'd think boys their age would have more stamina."

"Maybe you should give them some time off."

Donna looked up from the documents and stared at Lark as if she'd just suggested sending all three boys on a month-long trip to the moon. "How much time?" she asked, horrified at the mere thought of it.

"The weekend," said Lark decisively. "The *whole* weekend. Meaning they can sleep in, lounge in front of the TV, maybe even go out for Chinese food or to a movie. No rehearsals, no dance classes, no photo shoots."

Donna tugged off her mock-tortoiseshell reading glasses and let out a long rush of breath. "There's still so much to do," she muttered, "but I suppose if you think it's a good idea—"

"I think it's a great idea," said Lark. "They need to relax and have some fun."

Donna thought for a moment, returned her glasses to the bridge of her nose, and waved her hand. "Fine. Go tell them that as of right now, they're off the clock until Monday morning."

Smiling, Lark bent down and pressed a big kiss to the top of her mother's head. Then she bolted from the kitchen before Donna could change her mind.

In the family room she found the furniture restored to its usual arrangement. Ollie and Max were flopped on the sofa. Teddy was slumped in the oversize armchair, his long soccer player's legs stretched out on the ottoman.

Lark realized Donna hadn't been exaggerating. Abbey Road looked completely and utterly pooped!

"Great news," Lark announced.

"Another TV interview?" guessed Oliver.

"Better," said Lark, crossing the room to hand Teddy the folder. "My mom's just decided to give you all the whole weekend off!"

Oliver gave her a sideways look. "Please don't tease," he warned.

"I'm not teasing," Lark promised. "She realized that you've been working very hard and that you should be rewarded for it."

"Came to this realization all on her own, did she?" said Max with a grin.

"Well, she may have had a *little* coaxing from me."

"Thanks, Lark," said Ollie. "Really. I'd jump up and smother you with kisses of gratitude if only I had the energy."

"Bet she'd rather get kissed by Teddy," Max whispered loudly.

Luckily, Teddy was too engrossed in the contents of the folder Lark had given him to take note of the comment.

"I'm going up," Ollie decided, rising from the sofa with a wince. "My muscles are aching from all that dancing. I'm gonna soak in a hot tub for the next several hours."

"Sounds like a good idea," said Max, grunting as he stood up. "I call dibs on the Jacuzzi in the hall bathroom."

"You can have it," said Ollie wearily. "Not that I couldn't do with some whirlpool action, but the bath off my bedroom is a much shorter walk."

Together the boys hobbled out of the room.

"Wait," Lark called after them. "What about dinner? Fitzy just ordered pizza."

Max's voice floated back from the hall: "Too tired to chew!"

Lark sighed and turned to Teddy. "Well, I guess that means more pepperoni for us," she said cheerfully.

Teddy said nothing, just stared at the open folder in his lap.

"You wanna hear what you missed in school today?" Lark asked, hoping to break him out of his gloom. "There was major drama in the caf-a-gym-a-torium. In study hall, Melanie Cooper asked Henry Totten to find out at lunch if Scott McPhee liked her. Of course she made Henry promise not to let Scott know that she wanted to know, but instead of keeping it on the DL, Henry just blurted it out in the hot lunch line in front of everybody. Scott said he thought Mel was cute but he only liked her as a friend, which wouldn't have been so bad, except that Melanie was standing three people behind them in line! She heard everything and ran out crying."

Teddy continued to frown silently at the folder.

"You okay?" Lark prompted.

In response, Teddy held up a history paper. At the top, the teacher had scrawled a big red D–. Then he held up a math quiz marked with an F.

"Oh," said Lark, wincing. "Sorry."

Teddy shrugged. "That's what happens when you write a paper on the bus on the way to school the day it's due. And I didn't study for the math quiz at all because . . ."

". . . Because you've been so busy with Abbey Road," Lark finished for him. She knew the poor grades were all the more frustrating to Teddy because he was usually an honor student. It wasn't that he didn't understand the material, it was simply that he hadn't had time to give his schoolwork the attention it deserved.

Lark hated seeing him so unhappy. She hated it so much, in fact, that all she could think of was cheering him up, which was why she spoke without thinking.

"What are you doing tomorrow night?" she asked.

Teddy let out a grim chuckle. "Studying, what else? Well, that's what I was planning anyway. I figured the band would be rehearsing all day on Saturday, so I'd be stuck spending the night trying to catch up on schoolwork."

"But now that you've got the whole weekend off, you can study during the day, right?"

"I guess." Teddy looked at her curiously. "Why?"

"Because my dad's playing backup guitar for the Hatfields, right here in LA. I've got two tickets and I thought maybe you could come with me."

She realized with a thud of her heart that she had just asked Teddy Reese on a date!

CHAPTER FIVE

Lark still couldn't believe Teddy had said yes!

She'd awoken that morning to a flood of insecurity, fearing he'd only accepted because she'd put him on the spot, or worse, because he was afraid of insulting the daughter of the woman who was going to make him a star.

But when she remembered the smile on his face when he'd responded, "I'd love to go to a concert with you," her worries vanished into the excitement of planning what she was going to wear.

By six o'clock that evening she'd tried on everything in her closet—twice—and still hadn't settled on the perfect outfit.

This called for reinforcements!

Lark FaceTimed Mimi, who was also in the process of

getting dressed for a big night—her cousin's birthday party. She'd wrestled her long dark curls into a super-high pony, and was looking fabulous in her flowing boho blouse and black jeans.

Lark explained her predicament.

"Okay," said Mimi. "Pan the room."

"*What* the room?"

"Cinematography term. It means sweep the camera around to give me a panoramic view. Not too fast, though. I don't want to get motion sickness and puke on my new shirt."

Obediently, Lark aimed her camera and moved it in a slow arc around the room, which was strewn with clothing, so that Mimi could assess the situation.

"Stop!" cried Mimi. "There. The denim shirt."

Lark reached for the chambray blouse, which she'd flung over her desk chair earlier. "Got it," Lark confirmed, and continued to pan the room.

"There, hanging on the bed post. The white jeans with the torn knees."

Lark grabbed for the pants.

"I'm not seeing any cardigans," said Mimi. "Where's that boxy crocheted one?"

"That's the one thing that's still in my closet," Lark said, turning the camera lens back to herself.

"Here's what you do," said the extreme close-up of Mimi

on the phone screen. "Wear the white jeans with the denim shirt. Button it up and put on a bunch of necklaces, the chunkier the better. Then put the crocheted cardi over it and leave it unbuttoned."

"Perfect!" said Lark. "But what about shoes?"

"Well, since you're seeing a country band, your cowboy boots would be totally appropriate, but they might also be a little predictable."

"That's what I was afraid of," said Lark. "What about the Doc Martens the boys got me for Christmas?"

"OMG, those will be amazing," Mimi cried. "Now, get dressed and send me a selfie, just to be sure it all comes together."

"Thanks, Meems," said Lark.

Five minutes later she was taking a head-to-toe photo of herself in the full-length mirror. She texted it to Mimi and was rewarded with a reply that featured a thumbs-up emoji and the word "gorgeous" in all caps.

Thnx
Text me later want 2 hear all about the big date

Lark felt a quiver shoot up her spine from just reading the *d* word.

Not a date. Just friends she texted back.

> Ha ha whatevs!!! But u will let me know if that changes, right?! I'm ur bff so it's the law

A plethora of kissy-face emoji followed, then:

> Btw posted the video last night 52 likes and counting.

Having no idea what to say to that, Lark responded with the universal symbol for "I literally do not know what I'm feeling right now":

> : /

There was a brief pause, then a link to the YouTube page appeared on the screen.

Lark couldn't decide whether to watch it or not. On the one hand, she hadn't seen it with the music dubbed in and she was dying to know how it had turned out. On the other hand, if she hated it, her disappointment would ruin her mood for her night—*as friends*—with Teddy.

Stepping over the piles of discarded wardrobe items on her bedroom floor, she hurried to the living room. She hoped that Max, who'd vowed to spend his entire day off in front of the TV, would be there.

He was lounging in the overstuffed armchair with a bowl

of popcorn in his lap, watching some mindless throwback sitcom.

"Can you keep a secret?" she asked.

"'Course I can."

Lark thrust the phone into his hand. "Will you watch this video and tell me if it's terrible? But you have to be honest."

Max gave her a quizzical look, then tapped the link. When she heard the guitar intro to "Everything's Working Out," her belly flipped over.

"Oi!" Max's eyes went wide. "This is you."

"I know," Lark murmured. "*That's* the secret."

Suddenly, her voice came through the phone speaker as the lyrics began:

Everything was dark and tragic
Now the world is full of magic

Max was tapping his foot along with the music and smiling. At a couple of points he even laughed out loud, but not in a bad way.

When it was over Lark held her breath.

Max looked up from the phone screen and stared at her for such a long moment that she began to squirm in her flowery Dr. Martens.

"This is incredible," he said at last. "The song, the camerawork . . . You're brilliant!"

"Really?"

"Yes, really! It makes our new video look like trash, to be honest."

"Does it?"

"It does. You know I wouldn't lie to you about something this important. Don't you like it?"

"I don't know," Lark admitted. "I haven't seen it yet."

Max looked at her as if she'd grown a second head. "Well then get over here right this minute," he commanded.

Reluctantly, Lark went to stand behind the armchair as Max hit the Play arrow a second time. Watching over his shoulder, she felt herself blushing whenever her face appeared on the screen. But with every new verse, her nerves relaxed a bit. Max wasn't exaggerating; the video really *was* terrific. Mimi had truly outdone herself. And so, for that matter, had Lark—if she did say so herself.

"It's not bad, is it?" she said modestly.

"It's ace."

"And it's a secret," Lark reminded him. "So please don't tell my mom. Not yet anyway. Maybe not ever."

"What's that supposed to mean?"

"It means that Mimi and I have a deal. Please Max, don't tell anyone. Not even Ollie and Teddy."

"All right, then. I did promise." He handed her back her

phone, then kissed her on the cheek in a brotherly way. "You're a talented girl, Lark Campbell. I'm proud of you."

Then Donna's voice came up from the kitchen: "Lark! Time to go pick up Teddy."

Lark gave Max a grateful squeeze, then in a jangle of chunky necklaces, she hurried down the stairs.

✳

Teddy was waiting on his front porch when Donna's car pulled up. He was wearing a vintage Springsteen T-shirt, jeans, and a pair of dusty-gray chukkas, and as far as Lark was concerned, he looked perfect.

"Hi," he said, sliding into the backseat. "Thanks for picking me up, Mrs. Campbell."

"You're very welcome, Teddy." Donna smiled at him in the rearview mirror. "Just try not to scream too loud during the encores. We don't want you damaging those vocal cords."

In the front seat, Lark rolled her eyes, turned the car radio on low, and changed the subject. "Mom, where are the tickets and the backstage passes?"

"In my purse," said Donna, motioning to the giant designer tote, which most people would consider an overnight bag but for Lark's mother served as an everyday accessory.

Lark fished around until she found them. The tickets were ordinary enough, but the backstage passes were laminated cards, each on its own lanyard. Lark handed one to Teddy. They exchanged excited smiles.

"This is my first real concert," Teddy confessed. "Well, unless you count the time I saw the Squirmies when I was five. My kindergarten class went to see them for a field trip."

"I remember the Squirmies!" said Lark.

"Hey, maybe Abbey Road should do a cover of one of their hits," Teddy teased.

"You totally should," Lark agreed, grinning. "After all, 'My Hippo Has the Hiccups' is a classic."

"True," said Teddy. "But I'm partial to 'The Bubblegum Boogie,' myself. Talk about a great dance track."

Lark laughed.

"You know," said Donna. "That's not a bad idea."

"Mom!" said Lark. "You can't seriously want the band to remake a kiddie song!"

"Of course not," said Donna. "But I do think covering an actual pop classic could be very lucrative. Lots of new bands remake older hits. Getting the rights can be pricey, but it might be worth it. In fact, I think we should start investigating—"

She was stopped by the sound of a familiar voice filling the SUV. Ollie's voice!

It took only a split second for Lark to realize what she was hearing. Abbey Road's single, "Wounded Pride," was playing on the radio. It wasn't the first time they'd heard the song on the radio, not by a long shot. But that didn't make it any less cool. Feeling giddy, she reached for the radio button and pressed it until it was blasting at full volume.

Remember when you stood right by my side?
You liked my clothes, you dug my ride
You said you'd be true, but girl, you lied
Now all I've got is wounded pride.

When Lark turned to glance at Teddy he looked happier than he'd been in days; her heart soared.

They pulled into the parking lot just as the song finished. Donna drove them right up to the door of the concert venue.

"Your father will send someone to escort you to his dressing room after the show. You'll be meeting at the auditorium's south exit, but you'll need to have your badges visible or you won't be admitted backstage. So put them on now."

Lark frowned, but dutifully placed the nylon rope around her neck. She suspected Mimi would have a problem with this particular wardrobe choice—lamination was hardly stylish and the lanyard totally clashed with her necklaces.

"Have fun," said Donna as they got out of the car. "Oh, Lark . . . wait one second." She reached into the glove box and pulled out a brand-new baseball cap emblazoned with the distinctive Lotus Records logo. "It's for your father."

Lark felt a warm tingle in her belly. "A gift? From you to Daddy? That's so sweet."

"It's good business," Donna clarified. "On tour, Jackson's surrounded by music-industry types, so why not let him do a little advertising on my behalf?"

"Right," said Lark, her warm tingle changing to a pang of disappointment. "I should have known. Business."

Donna waved and drove off, and Lark shoved the brim of the cap into her back pocket. It created an unsightly bulge under her cardigan, another fashion faux pas of which Mimi would have vigorously disapproved.

Inside the arena, Lark and Teddy milled through the crowd to one of the many concession stands.

"What would you like?" Teddy asked as they took their place in line. "My treat."

"Oh, you don't have to do that," said Lark.

"I want to do it," Teddy insisted. "So, what'll you have?"

Lark peered over the heads of the people in front of them and considered the large, lighted menu mounted above the snack bar. "Popcorn, I guess."

"Great," said Teddy. "I'll get the supersize one and we can share. Anything to drink?"

"Cherry Coke, please."

As they waited to take their turn at the counter, Lark was aware that several people were eyeing her backstage pass enviously.

In front of them, three teenage girls were ordering candy bars, double-cheese nachos, caramel corn, and *diet* sodas. Lark and Teddy exchanged an ironic look and laughed.

Then a girl's voice from behind called something out to them that made Lark's stomach drop to the toes of her flowered boots: "Hey! I recognize you!" she said. "You're in that video!"

Lark's heart thudded. Was this really happening? Did the girl mean "Homesick," or was she referring to the "Everything's Working Out" video that Mimi had posted yesterday? In either case, "Songbird" was being picked out of a crowd! What should she say? How should she act? There was no way of knowing from the tone of the question whether this person liked the video or hated it.

"It is you, isn't it?" the girl persisted.

There was no point in avoiding it, so Lark took a deep breath and whirled to face her accuser—a pretty teenager with dark braids and a flannel shirt.

"Um . . . ," Lark began. "As a matter of fact, it is—"

"The keyboard player!" the girl cried, jumping up and down in her hot-pink cowboy boots. "It *is* you!"

Only then did it occur to Lark that she wasn't the only person in line who happened to be in a music video at the moment.

"You're part of that new British boy band," the girl gushed, shouldering a man in a leather vest to position herself beside Teddy. "Abbey Road, right? OMG, you guys are amazing. And you're even cuter in person!"

Teddy's cheeks were as pink as the girl's boots. Suddenly, everyone around them was whispering and pointing. Cell phones were being pulled out of purses and pockets as the concession-stand crowd eagerly searched for the video in question.

"Can I get a picture?" the girl asked, though it was clear she had no intention of waiting for an answer. She was already snuggling against Teddy and aiming her phone at them from an upward angle. "Smile, gorgeous!" she commanded.

Teddy smiled.

The girl snapped a selfie, checked the screen, then snapped another.

"Will you sign my program?" she asked.

Flustered, Teddy borrowed a pen from the snack-bar cashier and quickly scrawled his name across the front of the concert program the pretty girl had thrust at him.

"Thanks," she said, and jostled her way back to her original place in line.

"Next!" cried the counter clerk.

The eyes of the crowd continued to rake curiously over Teddy and Lark. The attention actually made Lark's skin itch. Teddy did his best to ignore the whispers and flashing cameras as he ordered the supersize popcorn and two sodas and they quickly made their escape.

"I can't believe I got recognized!" said Teddy, his expression a mix of shock and pride. "I mean, who expects to get noticed in a crowd this big?"

"Yeah, who would ever expect that?" Lark muttered, mortified. *Me, that's who.* She couldn't believe she'd been self-centered enough to think that the celeb-spotting had been directed at *her*.

"It was actually pretty cool," Teddy confessed. "But I hope it doesn't happen again tonight." He gave her a sweet smile. "I kind of wanted this d—" He stopped short and corrected himself. "This *night* to be just about us."

And back to the warm tingle! Lark thought her heart might actually burst. She was certain he had been about to say "date," and had only changed his mind because he didn't want to embarrass her by assuming they were more than friends.

They entered the arena and made their way to their seats, which were basically the best in the house. *Thanks, Dad!* thought Lark. She noticed a girl and her mother were pointing at Teddy and whispering.

"Here," said Lark, tugging the Lotus baseball cap out of her pocket and handing it to Teddy. "Put this on."

"Good idea." Teddy took the hat and pulled it down low over his forehead. "Check me out," he joked. "I'm incognito. Well, sort of, anyway. Let's just hope the lights go down soon."

"You should probably get used it," said Lark, serious now. "Once the album's released you're going to get even more attention."

They settled into their seats and Teddy placed the gigantic popcorn tub between them. Lark, who had spent so much time agonizing over her outfit that she'd forgotten to eat dinner, was starving. She reached for a handful of popcorn.

So did Teddy.

At the exact same moment.

Their fingertips touched, amid the warm kernels. It was all Lark could do to keep from jerking her hand out of the bucket in a panic. But to her surprise, Teddy let his fingers linger against hers

So she did the same.

We're almost holding hands, she thought, and in her mind, it sounded like the lyric to a song.

Then the lights dimmed and the crowd went wild.

The thrill was contagious. Lark and Teddy abandoned their handfuls of popcorn to join in with the cheering fans.

❋

The concert was amazing. The Hatfields' showmanship was exceeded only by their musical talent. Lark's favorite point in the show was when the lead guitarist waved her father up to the front of the stage to jam with him. The entire arena exploded in applause for Jackson. Lark stood on her chair and shouted, "Go, Daddy! You rock," at the top of her lungs.

Two and a half hours and three encores later, the band finally called it a night. Lark's voice was hoarse from cheering and singing along with the songs, all of which she knew by heart. Teddy had kept the yelling to a minimum as per Donna's instructions, but seemed to enjoy the show every bit as much as Lark did.

As they bumped and shuffled along with the stream of fans toward the south exit, Teddy turned to Lark with a guilty expression. "I used to think country music was only for cowboys and hillbillies. Barefoot guys strumming on a washboard, singing about the flat tire on their pickup truck, or their favorite hunting dog who ran away. I guess that was pretty narrow-minded of me, huh?"

"Yup," said Lark, grinning. "But you don't have to look so ashamed about it. Lots of people have silly ideas of what they *think* country music is." She shrugged. "Do you have a different opinion now?"

Teddy nodded. "Tonight's show made a believer out of me. Those Hatfields guys can really play!"

"And the lyrics weren't all about moonshine and coal mining," Lark teased.

"What's your favorite thing about country music?" Teddy

asked as they passed a vendor selling T-shirts, marked down to half what they cost before the concert.

"Other than the fact that it reminds me of home?" Surprisingly, no one had ever asked her that question before. She took a minute to think about it, going over all her favorite songs in her mind . . . the power of the words, the swell of the chords, the way a good song could get your toes tapping without you even realizing you were doing it . . .

"It's the simplicity that I really love," she said at last. "Country music is uncomplicated. It's real. And I love that the lyrics tell stories. Simple stories, with honesty and emotion. You can't help making a connection. It's just so . . . *welcoming*."

Teddy let the explanation sink in, then smiled. "I think it's cool that you can write in both styles—country and pop. I guess you're what's called a crossover artist."

"I'm just a girl with a guitar," Lark said with a shrug.

By the time they reached the south exit, the crowd had thinned considerably. A young man in a windbreaker with "Crew" printed on the back was waiting. He waved as they approached. "Lark Campbell?"

"That's me."

The crew member checked their passes and nodded. "I'm Clint," he said. "Right this way, please."

They followed Clint through a maze of concrete corridors until they reached the dressing-room area. The place was mobbed with other fans lucky enough to be wearing backstage passes. Music was playing, glasses were being raised, and photos were being snapped.

And there he was!

"Daddy!" Lark cried.

Jackson Campbell—who was chatting with a very pretty backup singer—turned in the direction of Lark's voice and his face lit up with joy. "There's my darling," he said.

The next thing Lark knew, the crowd was parting for her and she was running toward her father, flinging herself into his arms.

"You were amazing, Daddy!" she whispered into the scruff of his beard. "Real fine!"

"Well, thank you, Songbird," Jackson said, squeezing her tight. "I tried."

"But this beard has got to go!"

"We'll talk about that later," said Jackson, holding her at arm's length and studying her. "Now, let me look at you." He frowned. "Girl, what on God's green earth are you wearing on your feet?"

"Doc Martens," Lark explained sheepishly. "They're from London."

Jackson shook his head and clucked his tongue, pretending to be affronted. Then he hugged her again and they laughed. Out of the corner of her eye, Lark saw the pretty singer quietly take her leave.

Good, thought Lark.

Teddy joined them and held out his hand for Jackson to shake. "Hi, Mr. Campbell. I'm Teddy."

"Nice to meet you, son," Jackson said, sliding a look at Lark. "I remember you from the talent show. You and my Songbird were a big hit."

"He's the keyboard player for Abbey Road now," said Lark.

"Did somebody say 'keyboard player'?" came a jovial voice from the doorway of a nearby dressing room.

Lark turned to see a lanky man with long blond curls.

"This here is Garret Givens," said Jackson, smiling at the man who was now swaggering toward them. "He thinks the sun comes up just to hear him crow."

"That ain't so," Garret countered in a heavy Southern accent. "It comes up to hear me play the piano!"

"Give, this is my little girl," said Jackson, clapping Garret on the back. "I think I may have mentioned her once or twice."

"*Mentioned* her?" Garret Givens let out a bark of hearty laughter and smiled at Lark. "Heck, darlin', you're just about the only thing your daddy ever talks about. He's awful proud of you."

"I'm proud of him, too," said Lark.

"Boys! C'mon over here and meet Jackson's daughter."

The next thing Lark knew, all six members of the Hatfields were gathered around her, shaking her hand and giving her bear hugs. It was similar to being greeted by Ollie and Max, only with a lot more facial hair!

"When are you going to start touring like your daddy?" asked the drummer, who was the youngest Hatfield, and so ruggedly handsome that Lark found herself too tongue-tied to respond.

"Not until after she graduates from college," Jackson answered for her. "No show business for Lark until after she gets an education. And maybe not even then."

Tell that to Mimi, thought Lark.

When the introductions were over, the band members made their way over to a large table piled high with food: chicken wings, barbecued ribs, fried chicken, and chili.

Garret said to Lark, "Now then, what were you saying about a keyboard player?"

"I was saying that my friend Teddy plays in a band my mom's record label just signed." Lark motioned to Teddy. "He's super talented."

"Is he, now?" said Garret. He pointed to an electric keyboard across the room. "Why don't y'all come see if you can help me out with a new song I've been working on. It's about splitting up with my missus, because nothing sells like a country song about heartbreak!"

"Sure," said Teddy, his eyes lighting at the invitation. "That'd be great."

As Garret played the first few measures of his work

in progress, Jackson got right to the point. "Is he your boyfriend?" he whispered to Lark.

Lark blushed. "No!" she whispered back. "We're just friends. He's not my boyfriend."

Jackson raised his eyebrows and grinned. "But you wish he was, don't ya?"

More than anything, thought Lark, but she wasn't about to reveal that particular truth to her daddy. And since she couldn't bring herself to lie to him, she changed the subject. "What about that backup singer you were flirting with when I got here?" she challenged. "The one in the tight skirt and the fake eyelashes. Is she your girlfriend?"

Teddy was making some real improvements to Garret's composition; from the sound of Garret's appreciative chuckle, he was very pleased.

"She's a professional acquaintance," Jackson said (which Lark figured was the grown-up equivalent of "just friends"). "But even if Tonya and I *were* romantically involved, the difference is, I'm old enough to be in a relationship. You're much too young to have a serious boyfriend."

"Fine." Lark felt her mouth twisting into a pout. "But all I'm saying is that if you're going to be in a relationship, why can't it be with Mom? She's still single, you're still single—"

"Darlin'," said Jackson, sighing, "your mama and I just aren't gettin' back together. It's that simple."

"Simple like a country song," Lark grumbled, closing her eyes.

Suddenly, the melody Teddy was playing on the keyboard felt like it was swirling around in her heart, and words tumbled into her mind.

"Mr. Givens," said Lark, going over to the keyboard. "How about this . . ." She took a deep breath, forced herself to ignore the fact that she was surrounded by strangers, and began to sing:

I took that girl to be my wife,
We made our vows, and planned our life.
But dreams get broke, the pieces scatter,
I tell myself that it just don't matter . . .

Lark was surprised at how easily the words came, given her recent bout of writer's block. Maybe it was because this song didn't come with any expectations—whereas her mother was desperately hoping that Lark would come up with another big hit for Abbey Road.

Garret frantically scribbled Lark's words on a notepad. "Keep going," he said. "Just sing what's in your heart. And you"—he grinned at Teddy—"try picking up the tempo a little bit."

"Good idea," said Teddy.

Teddy adjusted the music's pace, playing the next verse with a faster beat. Lark lent her voice to the tune:

She and me weren't meant to be,
Now we're nothing but a memory.
We're doing our best to stay friends,
But heartache starts where our love ends…

When Lark finished, there was a round of heartfelt applause.

Jackson pulled Lark close. "That was beautiful, Songbird. I guess I didn't realize how much you're hurting. I'm so sorry about that, baby. Divorce hurts, don't it?"

"Divorce hurts," Lark echoed against his chest, then laughed in spite of herself. "I think we have our song title."

Garret wrote out the title and beamed at Lark. "I hope it ain't past your bedtime, little girl, because we're gonna need a bridge, a chorus, and at least three more verses."

As the fans and other guests dispersed, Lark, Teddy, Jackson, and Garret spent the next hour feasting on the remaining wings and ribs and working on the song.

It was the perfect ending to an incredible night.

When they'd finished, Garret Givens promised that the Hatfields would play the new song at their next show in Seattle.

"You two will both get a songwriting credit," Garret promised Lark and Teddy. "I'll get in touch with your mama about royalties later."

But Lark didn't care about the money. All that mattered was that her father would be playing and singing a song she had written for him. And for her. And for Donna.

A tribute to the family they once were and the new, slightly bruised but determined family they had become.

CHAPTER SIX

On Monday morning, Mimi came barreling down the seventh-grade hall, calling Lark's name. Lark laughed as Mimi skidded to a halt a split second before crashing face-first into Lark's open locker door.

"Wait until you see this!" said Mimi, whipping out her phone. "It's mind-boggling."

"What is?" asked Lark. "Did you get a personal invitation from Tim Burton to assistant direct his next movie?" She could think of nothing else that would have Mimi so excited.

Mimi was tapping her phone like a madwoman. "I was so busy over the weekend with the party and everything that I forgot to check, but when I looked this morning—"

"Miss Solis!"

The angry voice boomed down the hall, stopping a couple of skittish sixth graders in their tracks.

Lark and Mimi whirled to see Mr. Corbin, their history teacher, scowling at them.

"Miss Solis, haven't I told you repeatedly that phones are not to be used during school hours except in the event of an emergency?"

Mimi gulped. "Yes, sir."

"Is this an emergency?"

Lark slid a sideways look at her best friend, who seemed to be weighing up her answer. She wondered if Mimi and Mr. Corbin had the same definition of "emergency." For example, Christopher Nolan announcing that he was retiring from making movies might constitute a life-changing event in Mimi's mind, but it wasn't likely that Mr. Corbin would share her extreme distress over such news.

"No," said Mimi at last. "Not really. Just some really good news I wanted to share with Lark."

"Well, then," said Mr. Corbin, holding out his hand for the phone. "Miss Campbell will have something to look forward to at the end of the day. But for now, I'm confiscating your cellular device."

When Mimi looked as if she might protest, Lark subtly elbowed her in the rib cage. Mimi sighed and turned over her phone.

"You may pick it up in Principal Hardy's office after seventh period. Now get to class before the bell rings."

"Yes, sir," Mimi repeated, then leaned close to Lark and whispered, "Library. After fourth."

She was gone before Lark could respond.

✳

As cryptically instructed by her BFF, Lark reported to the library immediately following her fourth-period class. Luckily, it was lunch period, so she didn't have to worry about being late for anything. She did, however, have to worry about not having time to eat and missing out on whatever "delicacy" Fitzy had packed in her lunch bag that morning.

Mimi practically leaped out from behind the fiction shelves, grabbed Lark's elbow, and began dragging her toward the study carrels.

"You've gotta see this!" she whispered. "It's awesome."

"I've seen the library before, Meems."

"Ha, ha, very funny." Mimi pulled her along until they found a secluded spot near the back of the library. Then she reached into her backpack and pulled out a cell phone.

"I thought Mr. Corbin took your phone," said Lark.

"He did. This is Trevor Yoshida's. He let me borrow it." She shrugged. "He kinda likes me."

Lark gave her a look. "*Kinda?*"

"Well, maybe more than kinda," Mimi admitted, her fingers tapping the screen. "His password is 'Mimi.'"

Lark laughed, then jumped when a blast of music blared through the speaker of Trevor's phone. It was a song she recognized instantly—after all, she was the one singing it.

"Everything's working out . . ."

Every head in the library turned in their direction, including the librarian's.

"Shhhhhhh!"

"Sorry," Mimi whispered, deftly muting the video.

"Are you trying to get us expelled?" asked Lark.

"Of course not." Mimi rolled her eyes and handed the phone to Lark. "Look!"

Lark's gaze went straight to the little number in the right-hand corner beneath the video.

She gasped.

"I know, right?" said Mimi. "I only put it up a few days ago, and look at all those views and likes! And there's more." Flicking her finger over the screen, she scrolled down through the first several comments. "Check *this* out!"

Lark read the comment Mimi was pointing to. It was from someone called DBay and it said, "Songbird, you've got the goods. Gimme a shout ASAP. I'm at Zeitgeist Music."

"You think it's real?" asked Lark, a tremble shooting through her.

"I do," said Mimi, beaming. "I went on the Zeitgeist

website and it seems pretty legit. It says the CEO is a guy named Danny Baylor. Cool, huh?"

"Cool if it's the real deal," Lark conceded. "Creepy if it isn't."

"But I think it *is* the real deal," said Mimi, bouncing up and down. "Lark, some record executive wants you to give him a shout!"

Of course "giving a shout" to a perfect stranger was the last thing in the world Lark would ever do. But that didn't mean the interest wasn't flattering. A shriek that was part joy and part horror escaped her.

Again, everyone in the library whirled to glare at her.

"If you girls insist on making noise, you're going to have to leave," the librarian scolded from the circulation desk. "Other students are trying to study."

Embarrassed, Lark looked away from the librarian. Which was when she noticed that one of those "students trying to study" was Teddy.

"Put the phone away," Lark advised Mimi in a whisper. "It won't do much for your relationship with Trevor if you get *his* cellular device confiscated, too."

"Good thinking," said Mimi, quickly stuffing the phone into her backpack.

The girls made their way to Teddy, who was bent low over a science textbook.

"Hi," said Mimi.

Teddy kept his eyes on the book. "Look, I really appreciate your interest in the band, but I'm trying to study."

Lark felt stung. "Oh. Right. Of course. We'll leave you alone."

Teddy snapped his head up. His face brightened with an enormous smile. "Hey."

"Hey," said Lark. "Sorry. We didn't mean to bother you."

"It's okay, really," said Teddy. "*You're* not bothering me at all. It's just that kids keep interrupting me to ask me about Abbey Road, and wanting to know how it feels to be a star. So I haven't gotten any work done."

"Uh, what part of 'star' don't you understand?" said Mimi. "Who cares about getting schoolwork done?"

"Teddy cares," said Lark.

Mimi shrugged. "Why? He's on the verge of becoming a pop phenomenon. Most people in his position would drop out of school altogether."

Lark felt a stab in her gut. She hated the thought of Teddy not being in school anymore.

"That's definitely not an option," said Teddy with a chuckle. "My parents are super supportive of my music career, but they keep reminding me that 'fame is fickle' and 'the entertainment industry is risky.' They don't want me to be disappointed if the band doesn't last long. I know they're right—it's just the nature of the beast."

"Beast? What beast?" asked Mimi, confused.

"The boy-band beast," Lark clarified.

"I don't know what you're talking about," Mimi protested. "Oliver Wesley is definitely *not* a beast. Neither is Max!"

"It's just a figure of speech," said Teddy. "The point is, I really want to get my GPA back up to where it was before I joined the band, just in case. Stardom doesn't come with any guarantees."

Something suddenly occurred to Lark. "What about the tour? It's going to last three whole months! You're going to miss a lot of school while the band is on the road."

"I'm taking a leave of absence," Teddy explained. "The band's tutor is going to coordinate with my regular teachers so I can stick to the curriculum. The tour will be over in time for me to come back to school, at least for the month of June, and hopefully I won't be behind in my classes."

Lark was about to tell him she was impressed by that philosophy when his phone dinged, signaling a text message. He snuck it out of his pocket and kept it low, so the librarian wouldn't see it. "I'm usually not this sneaky, but your mom has a rule about being reachable at all times."

Lark sighed. "I'm very familiar with that rule."

Teddy checked the message. "It's from your mom's PR assistant, Julia," he said. "She says they need me at the house today after school for a photo shoot and to meet with a wardrobe consultant about what wear for the TV interview." He smiled. "So save me a seat on the bus."

Lark turned to Mimi. "Meems, you've got more fashion sense than anyone I know. You should come over and help. "

"I'm glad you suggested it," said Mimi. "Saves me from having to invite myself over. Because you know I'm not about to miss the opportunity to see Oliver modeling cool clothes."

"Well," said Lark, "we should let Teddy get back to his studying."

"Yeah," said Mimi. "Good luck with that whole education thing."

"Thanks," said Teddy, expelling a heavy breath. "I need it."

As they exited the library, Lark paused to glance back at Teddy, who was once again hunkered down over his textbooks. Would that be what she'd have to look forward to if she ever did decide to "give a shout" to the mysterious Danny Baylor, CEO of Zeitgeist Records? Pressure, stress, relentless fans, and the possibility of leaving school.

Of course it would. That was how fame worked.

And it didn't exactly sound like Lark's idea of a good time.

In fact, it sounded like torture.

CHAPTER
SEVEN

Lark's mind was preoccupied for the rest of the day. Knowing that a music executive (one who didn't just happen to be her own mother) thought she "had the goods" filled her with confidence. It was an entirely new feeling for Lark; she was used to doubting her ability to share her talent with an audience.

It occurred to her now, though, that maybe she'd been leaning a little too hard on that old "stage fright" excuse. After all, she'd survived the talent show, and she'd even improvised a bit backstage at the Hatfields' concert—unintentionally, of course, but she'd gotten through that too.

She was so lost in her thoughts that she almost didn't notice the note that landed on her desk in history class, from none other than Alessandra Drake. She turned to Mimi, who sat two desks away and looked as surprised as Lark. Lark gave her a look that said, *What should I do?*

Mimi shrugged. *Open it*, she mouthed.

Lark opened up the folded piece of paper carefully, as if it might explode.

Wanna go to the mall with me and Mel after school today? it said.

Lark blinked. This had to be a mistake. Ally must have misjudged her throw; maybe she'd been aiming for Josh Pell's desk. Josh was a skater dude who wore baggy pants and slouchy knit beanies, and although he didn't exactly strike Lark as the mall type, he was the only other official A-lister in the room and therefore the only person Ally ever communicated with during class.

But when Lark snuck a glance across the aisle, she saw that Ally was smiling at her, awaiting a reply.

Lark gripped her pen and held it poised above the creased paper. She stared at the unexpected invitation, written in Ally's loopy script.

Ally Drake wants me to go to the mall with her, she thought, imagining herself sauntering through the airy, fountain-dotted corridors of an upscale shopping plaza flanked by Ally and Mel. She saw glossy shopping bags swinging from their wrists, their hair bouncing on their shoulders as they flitted from store to store . . .

It wasn't until Lark realized she was picturing it all

happening in slow motion that she recognized how ridiculous it was.

Because Ally didn't want to be Lark's friend; she just wanted to get one degree closer to Abbey Road.

Thanks, but I can't, Lark wrote back. Then, with a grin she added, Mimi and I have plans to hang with Ollie, Max, and Teddy all afternoon.

This was absolutely true, of course, though it may have been a little mean to rub it in Ally's face like that. But it was far less unkind than Ally pretending to want to be friends with Lark when in truth her motives were purely selfish.

Lark folded the note and threw. It landed square in the center of Ally's desk.

Keeping her eyes on the front of the classroom, where Mr. Corbin was finishing up his lecture on the First Continental Congress, Lark heard the whispery crackle of the note being unfolded.

Part of her wanted to sneak a glance across the aisle to see the expression of shock on Alessandra's face. After all, getting rejected wasn't something that happened to her often. But another part of Lark was content to simply focus on her teacher's description of the events that had taken place at Carpenters' Hall in 1774.

Because she was beginning to understand that in the scheme of things, Ally Drake just wasn't that big a deal.

✳

Lark arrived home with Teddy and Mimi to find that the foyer had been set up as a makeshift photo studio, with cameras on tripods and umbrella-shaped light reflectors all over the place. Ollie was posing in front of a white backdrop, while a girl with blue lipstick held a light meter up to his chin. A guy with a makeup brush in one hand and another clamped between his teeth was dusting Ollie's cheeks with bronzing powder, while a woman wearing stiletto heels that looked like stilts fussed with his shaggy blond hair.

"Let's hurry it up, people," the photographer scolded. "He looks fabulous, now get out of the way so I can shoot him!"

The hair and makeup crew scattered and Lark watched as Ollie struck a pose.

"Perfect!" said the photographer, whose skinny jeans looked as if they'd been painted on him. "That's perfect. Now smile. No! Wait, don't smile."

Ollie put on a brooding expression.

"Excellent," cried the photographer. "Very enigmatic."

Very grumpy, thought Lark.

The explosive flash that followed nearly blinded her.

"Who's next?" the photographer barked.

"Max," said the male makeup artist, pointing in the direction of the family room. "But he's being difficult."

Teddy laughed. "This ought to be good."

Lark, Mimi, and Teddy watched as the girl with the blue lipstick stomped from the foyer to where Max was lounging on the family room sofa. She planted herself in front of him, but before she said a word, Max vehemently shook his head.

"We're not having this conversation again," he said firmly. "I already told you there is no way I'm letting you tweeze my eyebrows!"

"Tweezing is so last millennium!" said the girl. "It's all about waxing now."

"Tweezing, waxing," Max grumbled. "I don't care if you're planning to take a lawn mower to them, I meant it when I said nobody was touching my eyebrows!"

It was at that moment that he spotted the onlookers in the doorway and waved them over. "Can you believe this? She actually wants to melt hot wax and apply it to my face! What'll she do next? Put me on the rack and break my bones? Stick me in an iron maiden?"

"Isn't Iron Maiden a heavy-metal band from the eighties?" said Teddy.

Max chuckled, but stayed on topic. "Point is, she thinks she's got to resort to medieval torture to make me appealing," he said gruffly. "Tell them, Lark. I'm not *that* ugly!"

The makeup artist turned to Lark with an expectant look and Lark felt the shyness settle over her as if *it* were hot wax.

"He's not ugly," she managed to say. "Not ugly at all."

"I never said he was," the girl with the blue-tinted lips insisted. "He's adorable! His brows are just a little scraggly, that's all."

Lark resisted the urge to peer more closely at Max's eyebrows. She honestly thought he was perfect the way he was, but this girl was a trained cosmetologist, after all. She was about to suggest that Max just succumb to the grooming when Donna came thundering into the room.

"I can't believe it. Yolanda canceled!"

"Who's Yolanda?" asked Lark.

"Only the most sought-after stylist in Los Angeles," said Donna. "She just called to say she can't make it for the fitting. And after she sent over all these possible ensembles."

Only now did Lark notice that the room contained several rolling racks filled with clothing.

Mimi sauntered over to the racks and examined some of the outfits hanging from them. "Maybe that's not such a bad thing," she observed, eyeing a neon-green tuxedo. Next to it hung a pair of seersucker trousers, paired with a light-blue and pale-yellow argyle sweater and a seafoam-green button-down shirt.

"Preppy with a vengeance," she proclaimed, wrinkling

her nose in disgust. "Whoever wore this would look like human cotton candy."

Oliver plucked a fedora from the rack and set it jauntily on his head. "What do you think?" he asked, grinning at Mimi.

"You look absolutely *fedorable*," she said, quickly whipping out her phone and snapping a photo.

"How are we supposed to find a stylist on such short notice?" Donna muttered. "I booked Yolanda weeks ago."

"Mom, guess what!" said Lark. "I got an A on a short story I wrote for English."

Donna looked up from her phone, where she was Googling wardrobe consultants, and peered at Lark closely.

"I said, I got an A on my story," Lark repeated.

"Yes, yes, that's excellent, honey." She abandoned her Internet search and began to examine Lark's hair, then checked the condition of her nails. "Hmm. I wish I'd thought to schedule an appointment at the salon for you. You could use a little trim, maybe a manicure."

Lark looked at her strangely. "Why?"

"Why not?" Mimi joked.

Without another word about Lark's story, Donna left the room, her eyes glued to her phone as she continued to search for a stylist.

✳

After Max and Teddy were finished with their photo shoots, they all convened around the kitchen table to feast on Fitzy's latest creation: butterscotch-and-bacon blondies.

Lark was surprised to find the unexpected collision of sweet and savory oddly satisfying. She and Mimi each had one large blondie, but Donna recoiled at the thought of such a high-calorie snack. The boys had no such concerns and scarfed down the remainder of the batch.

"I suppose we're lucky to have dodged the green-tuxedo bullet," Donna said, sipping the kale smoothie Fitzy had whipped up for her. "I haven't been able to find another wardrobe consultant on such short notice. So we still need to find great outfits for you three to wear for the *Rise and Shine* interview tomorrow morning."

"The thing is," said Max, brushing blondie crumbs from his chin, "you've always said that Abbey Road's vibe should be that we're just normal, ordinary guys."

"Right," said Ollie. "So why don't we just do what normal, ordinary guys do when they want to look good?"

"What's that?" asked Donna.

"They go to the mall," said Max. "And Lark and Mimi can come along to help us shop."

Donna frowned. "I suppose we don't have much choice," she said, digging into her purse to fish out the Lotus Records company credit card. She handed it to Lark. "One outfit per band member, plus something cute for you."

"Me? Really?" Lark was thrilled; she hadn't treated herself to new clothes in a while. "Thanks, Mom."

A few minutes later they all climbed into the SUV, headed for the mall.

"Just normal, ordinary guys," joked Ollie. "Hanging out at the mall. What could be more typical than that?"

At that moment, Abbey Road's hit single, "Wounded Pride," came on the radio. As the group sang along to their own voices, Lark couldn't help but smile. There was nothing ordinary about these boys, and all thoughts of "typical" went right out the window as soon as they began to sing.

CHAPTER EIGHT

Donna dropped them off at the main entrance to the mall and told them she'd be back to pick them up in three hours.

"Let's start at Tristan and Gabriel," Mimi suggested. "It's the coolest shop in the mall."

Lark had never been to T&G, since it was a men's clothing establishment, but she'd walked by its windows many times before. They catered to the very affluent and fashion-forward, with a mix of trendy and classic apparel from all the best designers.

Inside T&G, a waifish salesgirl with plump, red-glossed lips approached them.

"Welcome to Tristan and Gabriel. May I help you?"

"Yes, you may," said Ollie, turning on the charm. "I would like an outfit that will make me completely irresistible to all women everywhere, starting with you."

The girl gave him a sultry smile. "Oh, you don't need an outfit for that," she replied in a husky voice.

Lark rolled her eyes.

As Ollie prepared to enter the girl's phone number into his cell, Max clapped him on the shoulder. "Easy, mate. We've got work to do." Then Max turned to the girl. "We've got a rather important event tomorrow, miss. It's casual, but we want to look our best. Not too flashy, but not dull and boring either."

"I doubt very much you three could ever be dull or boring," the salesgirl purred flirtatiously.

Mimi stepped forward, taking charge. "If you'll just set up some dressing rooms for them, I'll handle everything else."

With that, she began searching the shelves and racks, picking out shirts, sweaters, jeans, and trousers. Lark followed along, helping to carry things.

Fifteen minutes later, each member of Abbey Road was behind a closed changing-room door, trying on the outfits Mimi had chosen.

Max emerged first, in a snug-fitting plum-colored T-shirt made of buttery soft cotton. The neckline was a deep V, showing off his smooth, dark skin and a bit of his well-defined physique. The color was perfect for his British-Caribbean complexion, and the way the fabric clung to him really highlighted his dancer's muscles. He'd also put on a pair of gray jeans, which Mimi commanded him to roll.

"Make it a big fold, not a skinny cuff," she directed.

Max did as he was told.

Oliver was utterly in his element; he kept popping in and out of the dressing room, soaking up the admiration of the first salesgirl and two of her colleagues, who had by now heard about the pair of super-gorgeous Brits. Ollie modeled three separate outfits, all of which complemented his blond hair and blue eyes.

When he emerged for the fourth time he was dressed in a crisp white button-down shirt under a relaxed-fitting blazer the color of oyster shells. Dark denim jeans completed the outfit.

"That's the one!" said Lark. It was smart but not stuffy, and perfect for the band's charismatic front man.

"I agree," said Mimi. "We'll take it."

"What about shoes?" asked the salesgirl with the red lip gloss, deferring to Mimi's expertise.

"Brogues," said Mimi decisively. "Caramel-colored. Wing-tip. Oh, and grab a pair of boots for Max and some surf-style sneakers for Teddy. Black-and-white check, if you have them."

The girl nodded and hustled off to the shoe department.

Lark noticed Max sneaking a look at the price tag on the

plum T-shirt. When he saw the numbers, he looked positively shocked. "I'm used to buying my clothes at the discount shops," he confided to Lark quietly. "This is a ridiculous amount of money to pay for a T-shirt. It's made of cotton, not gold."

"It is kind of crazy," said Lark. "But don't worry. Lotus is paying."

Max gave her a grateful smile, but he still looked uncomfortable at the thought of wearing such overpriced clothes.

Finally Teddy stepped out of his dressing room.

Lark had to stop herself from gasping out loud. He looked amazing, in a pair of torn jeans and a sleeveless, surf-inspired tee.

"What do you think?" asked Teddy.

"You're perfect," said Lark, then hastily added, "the outfit. It's perfect on you."

Teddy reached back into the dressing room and pulled out a brightly colored Hawaiian shirt, still on the hanger. It had little neon-colored palm trees and surfboards printed all over it.

Holding it up to Mimi, he asked, "Were you serious about this?"

Mimi grinned. "I figured since you're the Californian component of the band, you might as well look the part. It's supposed to be ironic."

Teddy eyed the shirt uncomfortably. "Any chance we can be ironic without being so . . . colorful?"

"I think the Hawaiian shirt is a little too much," said Lark gently, so as not to hurt Mimi's feelings. "But wait . . ." She dashed away from the dressing area to a rack of lightweight hoodies she'd noticed on the way in. After a quick search she found what she was looking for and brought it back to Teddy. "This still has the surfer vibe Mimi has in mind, but it's a little less . . . um . . . colorful."

Teddy slipped into the sweatshirt, which was a gorgeous blue a few shades softer than his eyes. He looked incredible. And more importantly, comfortable.

"We have a winner," Mimi declared.

The final selection was a cool fedora for Ollie.

As the boys changed back into their own clothes, Lark and Mimi brought their purchases to the cash register.

Lark shook her head and smiled. "Meems, I'm impressed. If you weren't so determined to become a filmmaker, I'd say you've got a real future as a personal shopper."

"I'm glad you feel that way," said Mimi. "Because now it's your turn."

❋

As they made their way through the mall, Lark became aware of people pointing to the boys and whispering. She was about to mention this and suggest they go home before they caused a riot, but Mimi was steering the group into a boutique called Wish List.

Lark, who preferred worn jeans and flannel shirts, had never shopped there before, but judging by the window display of flouncy skirts, flirty dresses, and filmy blouses, the place was a fashionista's fantasy.

As they filed into the store, all heads turned in their direction. The clerks and the shoppers—mostly teenage girls—stopped in their tracks to stare at Teddy, Max, and Ollie.

Lark felt an unreasonable surge of jealousy as a pretty blond girl holding a bundle of sundresses batted her eyes at Teddy.

"Good thinking, Mimi," said Ollie, ruffling her hair, then running a hand through his own. "We can find some cool threads for Lark and drum up fans at the same time."

Mimi directed Lark to a row of fitting rooms, which had pink paisley curtains instead of doors. There was a large, lavender-upholstered ottoman for the boys to lounge on.

"Be right back," said Mimi. As she spun on her heel and dove into the racks, it was clear she was a girl on a mission.

Ollie plopped down on the ottoman, then opened the round cardboard hatbox his fedora had come in. He placed it on his head and checked his look in the mirror. "I think this might become my trademark," he said, winking.

Max rolled his eyes.

Moments later Mimi returned with an armful of clothing. "Start with these."

Obediently, Lark took the pile and closed the curtain. She felt a flood of terror when she pulled off her jeans and realized that she was standing there in her "knickers" (as Ollie would say) with nothing but a flimsy piece of pink fabric between her and Teddy. She quickly pulled a yellow striped dress over her head, fumbled with the side zipper, and stepped through the curtain.

"Sweet," said Max.

"Gorgeous," said Ollie.

"Pretty," said Teddy.

But Mimi shook her head. "Take it off. You look like you're wearing one of Fitzy's aprons."

Lark retreated into the dressing room and shed the yellow dress. Next up was a clingy pencil skirt in royal blue and a black crop top that revealed a little too much bare skin for her taste. She pulled back the curtain to show the others.

"Sweet," said Max.

"Gorgeous," said Ollie.

"Pretty," said Teddy. Although this time Lark thought she noticed a slight blush on his cheeks.

"I like it," said Mimi, tilting her head this way and that. "But I don't think it's what your mom had in mind. Try the romper."

"The what?"

"That little one-piece playsuit thingy," said Mimi, pointing to the article of clothing in question. "It's shorts and a top in one. They're attached."

"Sounds like a real timesaver," Ollie quipped. "Unless of course you need to go to the loo in a hurry."

This earned him a smack in the head from Max. Teddy laughed.

Once again, Lark ducked behind the paisley curtain. She took the romper off the hanger and smiled. It was actually supercute; the fabric was a raspberry-and-white triangle print. The upper half was a modest tank style, separated from the bottom part by an elastic waistline with a raspberry sash. The shorts were loose-fitting and modest in length—definitely not as skimpy as the pencil skirt. The hemline of the shorts featured a pretty white lace ruffle.

Lark swept the curtain aside. The goofy smile on Teddy's face was the best compliment Lark could have hoped for.

"I'll take it!" she said. Then she closed the curtain and broke into a happy dance.

✳

Lark was so delighted with her purchase that she'd forgotten all about her fears that the boys might be on the verge of causing a real stir.

Until they exited the store.

The screaming started as soon as Ollie emerged from

Wish List with his new fedora perched on his head. The volume rose as Max and then Teddy joined him.

"Uh-oh," said Lark. "I was afraid of this."

Without warning, a girl lunged forward and threw her arms around Ollie's neck, hugging him as if they were long-lost friends reuniting after years apart.

"I love Abbey Road!" she squealed.

"Hey!" cried Ollie. "American girls certainly are friendly, aren't they?"

"Maybe a little too friendly," said Max as two girls began tugging on the sleeves of his shirt. Lark gasped when she heard a ripping sound and saw one of the sleeves come away in the girl's hand.

"Good thing it wasn't the expensive new one!" Ollie joked.

"This isn't funny," said Max. "We need to get out of here."

"I agree," said Teddy, sounding wary. "But how do we do that?"

Ollie laughed as a second girl ran up and stole the hat right off his head. "We do what the Beatles did in the opening scene of *A Hard Day's Night*," he told Teddy. "We run!"

Ollie, Max, and Teddy took off at a sprint, with Lark, Mimi, and thirty screaming fans hot on their heels.

Ollie led the way to the food court, but that was a dead end. They dashed through a high-end department store, then back out onto the main concourse. From there they raced down the escalator, which slowed the fans down slightly. But the girls, who were screaming the boys' names, still would not give up the chase.

"Now what?" Max panted.

"Look!" said Mimi, pointing. In the center of the glass-roofed atrium stood a beautiful baby grand piano. Lark knew from her occasional shopping trips that a tuxedo-clad pianist was brought in on the weekends to entertain mall patrons with lilting strains of classical music. But today, the piano was silent.

"I have an idea!" said Mimi. She turned to their pursuers, who were clambering off the escalator, and held up both hands. "Stop!" she commanded. "I have a proposition for all of you!"

"What's she talking about?" Teddy whispered to Lark.

Lark shrugged. She couldn't even begin to guess what Mimi had in mind.

"We know you love Abbey Road," Mimi continued. "But chasing them through the mall like this is ridiculous."

"That's easy for you to say," one girl shouted back. "You're friends with them!"

"Here's the deal," said Mimi. "If you promise to stop chasing Ollie, Max, and Teddy, they'll do a concert for you right here, right now. For free!"

This announcement elicited loud screams from the crowd.

"Sounds like they're down with that," said Ollie, smiling at his bandmates. "You blokes up for it?"

"I'm up for anything that will get me out of this mall in one piece," said Max.

"Me, too," Teddy agreed.

"Well, then . . ." Ollie gave Teddy a nudge toward the piano. "Let's get this party started, shall we?"

With the eager eyes of their fans upon him, Teddy approached the sleek black instrument, placed his fingers on the keys, and played a handful of notes. Lark recognized the tune immediately—as did the audience, who let out a cheer.

Oliver tossed the now-empty hatbox to Max, who began drumming on it like a bongo in time with Teddy's piano playing.

Ollie spun to the center of the atrium as if it were the stage at the Hollywood Bowl and began belting out the lyrics to "Wounded Pride." Thanks to the atrium's top-notch acoustics, his silky voice flooded the mall despite the absence of a microphone.

Mimi whipped out her phone and began to record the impromptu concert, leaping up on nearby benches and even crouching under the piano to get the best camera angles.

I felt like I stood out from the crowd
'Cause I had you, and I felt so proud

You said you'd be true, but girl, you lied
Now all I've got is wounded pride.

By now, a big crowd had gathered. Most of the girls were singing along. When Ollie made eye contact with one of them, she screamed and nearly fainted.

"Lark," Ollie called. "We need backup vocals!"

Lark shook her head. No way was she going to sing in the mall in front of all these strangers!

But when she glanced at Teddy, he smiled and waved her over. A nervous thrill shot up Lark's spine. Summoning her courage, she ran over to join him at the piano, where she smoothly harmonized along to the song.

Mimi zoomed in for a close-up of Lark and Teddy at the piano.

When Max abandoned his hatbox drum to show off his dance moves, the crowd responded with shrieks of delight. Lark recognized some of the choreography Jas had been teaching the boys, but Max threw in some cool pop and lock moves that were all his own. As the song reached its crescendo, Max really amped things up by executing a series of flawless backflips across the atrium's floor.

When they finished the song, the applause was almost deafening. It seemed as if the entire mall was chanting, "AB-BEY ROAD! AB-BEY ROAD! AB-BEY ROAD."

Mimi turned in a slow circle, filming the crowd as they cheered.

Ollie bowed. Max did a funky spin. Teddy waved to the fans.

And Lark drank it all in, beaming with pride.

CHAPTER NINE

The next morning, the boys were up before the sun to prepare for the *Rise and Shine* interview. Because of the early start, Teddy had slept over on the spare bed in Max's room. No matter how deeply Lark burrowed under the covers or grasped her pillow over her head, she couldn't tune out their voices as they talked excitedly about making their television debut.

Then, the doorbell rang. Lark could hear Donna telling the makeup artist and hairstylist to set up in the kitchen.

From under her pillow, Lark groaned. A makeshift salon in the kitchen would mean no breakfast. Unless Fitzy decided to get really creative and give new meaning to the term "pancake makeup."

She was just drifting back to sleep when her bedroom door opened and her mother came barreling in. "Lark, what are you doing?"

"Sleeping. Trying to, anyway."

"You should be up and dressed already!"

"Why? School doesn't start for hours."

"Not for school. For the interview with *Rise and Shine*. So come on, darling . . . rise and shine!"

It was a moment before Lark's groggy mind was able to fully process what her mother was saying. When she understood, she sat bolt upright. "Mom, I am *not* going to be part of this interview!"

"Of course you are," said Donna breezily. "The segment is called 'At Home with Abbey Road.' Well, you're part of being at home. So get dressed."

Lark leaped out of bed. "I can't believe you are springing this on me now!"

"I'm not springing anything on you. I assumed you knew. Why else would I buy you a brand-new outfit?"

Lark's anger flared. "Oh, I don't know . . . maybe to celebrate the A I got in English? Or maybe just because I'm your kid and I haven't gotten any new clothes in ages?"

Donna knit her brows. "I wasn't aware you expected to be rewarded for doing well in school."

"I don't, but—"

"And as far as being my kid is concerned, well, I should think that 'my kid' would understand the financial burden I'm under at the moment and know that buying expensive new clothes based only on the fact that we share DNA is not presently in our budget." Donna shook her head sadly. "I've said it a million times, Lark—everything I do for Lotus Records, I do for you! Lotus is our family business, mine and yours. Someday, the good Lord willing, it will be yours and your children's. But that's not going to happen if I don't continue to work my butt off to make Abbey Road a success. And I'm sorry, but I don't think it's so unreasonable to expect a little cooperation from you."

Lark didn't know what to say. Her eyes flickered to the window, where pale streaks of sunlight were just appearing beyond the palm trees.

"I know how much being in the spotlight frightens you," Donna went on, "but here's a news flash, honey: I'm scared, too. I'm scared of losing everything I've worked for, and of not being able to put a roof over your head. But when I have to choose between giving in to those fears and behaving like a responsible adult, responsibility is going to win every time."

"I never said you weren't responsible," Lark offered lamely. "Fine, I'll do the interview. But Mama, I just want to stay in the background. Please don't let the TV people fuss over me."

"That seems like a fair compromise," said Donna, smiling as she glanced at the pink-and-white romper draped over Lark's desk chair. "Seems a shame, though, that such a cute outfit and such a pretty and talented young lady aren't going to get a little air time."

"That's the deal, Mama," said Lark firmly. "Background or nothing."

"Background it is," Donna agreed. "I'll tell Bridget to just pretend that you're a very leggy lamp."

"Good. This should be about the band, anyway."

"I suppose that's true," said Donna. "Now hurry and get dressed. If you're downstairs in ten minutes, there might be time for the hair and makeup girls to give you a little dolling up."

"Mama . . ." Lark folded her arms and gave her mother a warning look.

"It was just a thought." Donna headed for the door, then turned back and gave Lark a smile. "And for what it's worth . . . ," she said softly, "it was real nice to hear you call me Mama again."

✳

Lark hurried downstairs in her new outfit to find the house overrun with producers, production assistants, and camera crew. Bridget Burlington-Carzinski was in the living room, where she had the boys lined up on the couch.

When Max joked, "We look like those 'hear no evil, see no evil, speak no evil' monkeys," Oliver immediately pressed his hands to his ears, Teddy covered his eyes, and Max clapped his hands over his mouth. This had Lark and the whole crew chuckling.

"Save it for when the cameras are rolling," Bridget said, unamused. "We'll ask you a series of questions," she explained, flipping through a stack of blue index cards. "After that you can give us a tour of the house. Show us where you rehearse, where you hang out, where you sleep."

"My room's a bit of a shambles," Max admitted sheepishly. "Didn't have time to make my bed."

"That's perfect!" Bridget assured him. "The fans will love it. One glimpse of the rumpled bed linens that the world's cutest drummer slept in will have teenage girls from coast to coast swooning into their breakfast cereal."

Teddy frowned. "What about me? I don't live here."

"Hmmm . . ." Bridget checked her index cards. "In your case, we'll just talk about how you became part of the band." She blinked her false eyelashes and again consulted her notes. "How *did* you become part of the band?"

"Lark made it happen."

"Lark? What's a lark?"

Lark, who'd been lingering nervously in the doorway, stepped forward. "I'm a Lark," she said. "Just pretend I'm a lamp."

Bridget looked at Lark as if she were a bit touched in the head.

"I'm Donna's daughter. I go to school with Teddy, and when the original keyboardist left, I suggested Teddy take his place."

"That's not in my cards," said Bridget.

"But it's how it happened," said Teddy.

"Right," said Max. "Lark saved the band. Without her there'd be no Abbey Road."

One of the PAs called out, "Ten seconds."

"Places," the segment producer instructed.

The boys sat up straighter on the sofa. Lark couldn't help feeling proud of them. Ollie in his blazer, Max in his plum-colored T-shirt, and Teddy in his pale-blue hoodie—they looked exactly like the superstars they were about to become.

Bridget waved Lark toward the arm of the sofa. "Perch there," she commanded.

"Perch?" Lark echoed.

"Unless you'd rather stand on the end table," Bridget said in a snippy tone. "Since you seem to be under the impression that you're a piece of furniture."

Obediently, Lark perched. But she made a mental note to inform Mimi that Bridget Burlington-Carzinski was a lot snarkier in person than she was on TV.

"Five seconds," the PA alerted them. "Four . . . three . . . two . . ."

"Welcome to 'At Home with Abbey Road'!" Bridget flashed a blinding smile at the camera. "These three young men are taking the music world by storm! They currently have the number-one single on the iTunes charts; their first album, *British Invasion*, will be released in February; and they're about to embark on a multicity US tour. Not bad for three guys who aren't old enough to drive yet!" She mugged to the camera, clearly pleased with her joke. "Boys, would you like to introduce yourselves to our audience?"

Ollie gave the camera his most disarming smile. "Hi, I'm Oliver Wesley, but you can call me Ollie. I like long walks on the beach, quiet evenings at home—"

"And giving cheeky answers to TV interviewers," Max interrupted, chuckling as he threw a playful elbow to Ollie's ribs.

"He's right," Ollie confessed, grinning. "I've never spent a quiet evening at home in my life."

Bridget let out a trill of laughter and gestured to Max.

"I'm Max Davis, and I want to give a shout-out to my family back in London." He waved at the camera lens. "Hi, Mum, Dad. Hey, Anna."

Bridge pounced on this. "Anna?" she prompted, with a hungry look in her eyes. "Your girlfriend?"

Max laughed. "Little sister."

"Ahhh." Bridget nodded as if she'd just gotten Max to reveal a closely guarded secret. Then she pointed to Teddy.

"Hey. I'm Teddy, and I'm—"

Bridget cut him off, turning a knowing look to the camera. "Here's something I just learned," she gushed, "that I bet you fans out there don't know. Teddy wouldn't be a member of the band—in fact, there wouldn't even *be* a band—if it weren't for this lovely young lady right here."

A nod from the producer sent the camera swinging away from Bridget's smiling face . . .

. . . and focusing right on Lark!

The first thing that popped into Lark's head was an image of her nine-year-old self at the Nashville Fourth of July parade, quivering with panic as she approached the bandstand to sing the national anthem.

"O-oh, say . . . can . . . you . . . seeeeee . . ."

In her mind's eye she could picture the faces of her friends and neighbors, and she could hear the music being played by the high school marching band. She recalled the horrible sensation of her knees going weak and then . . .

Crash!

She felt herself falling, her forehead clonking against the heavy metal base of the standing mic.

"Lark?" Bridget Burlington-Carzinski's voice sliced through the memory. "I asked if you could tell us how you single-handedly saved the band."

"Um . . . well . . . you see . . ." Lark swallowed hard, her eyes boring into the camera lens as if she were staring into the jaws of a vicious mythical beast.

"T-Teddy plays the piano."

Bridget's smile tightened. "I think we're all aware of that."

"Right. Of course. Y'all know that."

"Y'all?" Bridget leaped on the word like a tiger pouncing on a kill. "Is that a Southern drawl I detect?"

Lark nodded.

"So you're not from LA originally?"

Lark shook her head.

"Well, then this has to be doubly thrilling for a little country girl like you," Bridget prompted. "Living in Los Angeles *and* sharing your home with handsome British pop stars. It must be very exciting."

Lark gulped down her terror. "It's real exciting," she managed to croak, even as the light reflecting off Bridget's gleaming teeth threatened to blind her.

"Now, tell me, Lark . . . ," Bridget cooed, leaning forward as though to receive the juiciest secret in the universe. "Tell *America* . . . which one of these dreamy singing sensations do you have a crush on?"

The question hit Lark like a slap—a calculated, sneaky slap—and suddenly it was the Fourth of July all over again. She sensed her consciousness draining away; her body was getting incredibly light, as if it were filled with air instead of bones. Suddenly she felt Teddy's hand, reaching up to take hers. Hidden behind the throw pillow that rested against the sofa arm on which Lark was perched, his fingers wrapped around her trembling ones, just tightly enough to pull her back from the brink.

"Speaking of crushes," said Teddy, so smoothly that Bridget didn't even realize her ambush had been interrupted, "we've started working on our next single. It's a ballad called 'Crush on Me, Crush on You,' and we think it's going to be a big hit."

Out of the corner of her eye, Lark saw Ollie and Max shooting puzzled looks at Teddy. This, she knew, was due to the fact that no such song existed.

"An exclusive!" said Bridget, delighted. "Will you sing a bit of it for us? I'd love to hear it."

"I'd love to hear it, too," Ollie murmured through a crooked grin.

Teddy took a deep breath and began to sing, "*Girl, I'd never make you rush, but I've got a major crush. I heard a rumor . . . hope's it true, do you crush on me like I crush on you?*"

Max's eyebrows rose. Ollie's mouth dropped open. They both looked very, very impressed.

Lark felt the melody wrap around her heart, just like Teddy's hand had wrapped around her fingers. The tune was sweet and simple with a surprisingly country feel.

"Sounds like a surefire hit to me," said Bridget, aiming her smile at Ollie. "Now, let's talk to lead singer Oliver Wesley."

The lens that had been trained on Lark and Teddy shifted to zoom in for an extreme close-up of Ollie. Lark took advantage of the change in camera angle to slip quietly off the sofa and tiptoe out of the living room.

The minute her feet hit the floor of the foyer, she ran.

✳

"Tell me the truth. Did I make a complete fool of myself?"

"Of course not!"

"You're just being nice," Lark groaned. She was in her bedroom, frantically getting ready for school while Face-Timing Mimi. Unzipping the romper had been more of a challenge than she'd anticipated and now she was in danger of missing the bus.

"I'm not." Mimi, who was at the breakfast table, was battling her brother Jake for the last of the Froot Loops. "I mean, I'm not gonna lie . . . for half a second there, you looked like you might pass out, but I doubt anyone noticed but me!"

"She's right," said Jake, poking his face into the frame. "Everybody else was too busy staring at those long legs of yours!"

"Ewwww! Shut up!" said Mimi, shoving him aside and losing the last of the cereal in the bargain. "You're so not allowed to flirt with my best friend."

Lark waited until Jake had left the Solises' kitchen, laughing. "Do you think he has a point?" she asked. "Not about my legs, but about 'everybody.' Do you think a lot of kids from school were watching?"

Mimi shrugged. "Probably. It's a popular show. Anyway, there's nothing you can do about it now, right? So forget it. And think about this . . . right before you called, I checked the number of likes for 'Everything's Working Out.' You're up to eighty-eight thousand!"

"Am I supposed to think that's good news or bad news?" Lark asked glumly.

"Good news! Duh!" Mimi said, giggling. "Gotta go. See you on the bus."

CHAPTER TEN

The rest of the school week went by quickly enough. Lark did have to field a few comments about her appearance on *Rise and Shine* (all friendly and positive—except for "Way to freeze up on national television," which came, not surprisingly, from Ally Drake). But most of the attention went to Teddy. And most of the interest was in the song "Crush on You, Crush on Me."

To be honest, Lark had a few questions about *that* herself; problem was, she didn't have the nerve to ask them.

On Saturday, when Jas came to rehearse the boys (minus Teddy, who simply had too much schoolwork to catch up on), Lark decided to make herself scarce. She stayed in her room for the majority of the day, first getting her homework out of the way, and then working on a new song her mother had commissioned her to write.

As always, Lark could hear, even *see* the melody in her head. But as far as the lyrics went, it seemed as if the only thing she could nail down was the title: "Holding My Hand." She hated to admit it, but for the first time since she'd started writing songs, she was having trouble turning feelings into words.

"Okay," she said aloud, flopping down on her bed, pen poised above her songwriting journal. "What rhymes with 'hand'?"

Band. Understand. Make a stand. This land is your land. Your wish is my command. Teddy joined up when Aidan got canned.

"Ugggh!" She fell back into her pillows and let out a long, exasperated sigh.

Her writer's block was worse than ever! For Lark, not being able to write was like not being able to breathe. She needed to create songs . . . it was how she expressed herself, how she made sense of the world, or at least how she coped with the world when it was *not* making sense. Not being able to release the music that was swirling around inside of her was a horrible feeling . . . like desperately needing to sneeze and not being able to!

To make matters worse, this song had a lot riding on it. Donna had trusted her to write Abbey Road's next single, and Lark was sick over the possibility that she might let her mother and the boys down.

But nothing was coming together, despite the fact that the memory of Teddy's hand touching hers was so vivid that every time she looked at her hand she expected to find his fingers still wrapped around hers.

Maybe the trouble was that it was *too* vivid. Maybe she just needed a little distance from the memory before she could turn it into a song.

Distance and a hot fudge sundae.

Downstairs was shockingly quiet. Jas had gone, Donna was working in her home office, and the boys were out in the yard, kicking the soccer ball around.

Lark made her way to the kitchen, where she found Fitzy digging through the vegetable bins in the fridge.

"Let me guess," said Lark, smiling. "You're making lemon-lima-bean tarts again."

"No," said Fitzy. "Those weren't exactly a hit."

"Well, c'mon," said Lark, sliding onto one of the stools at the breakfast bar. "Anything that has lima beans as a primary ingredient is bound to fail."

"I suppose," said Fitzy, not the least bit insulted as she turned away from the fridge with an armful of carrots, celery, and onions. These she dumped into a colander in the sink and rinsed vigorously. "Which is why tonight I'm sticking to the classics and relying on an old favorite: homemade vegetable soup."

"Sounds delicious," said Lark. "But would you mind if I made myself a sundae to tide me over until suppertime?"

"The boys polished off the ice cream about an hour ago. But I could pour a little chocolate sauce over the cauliflower I was going to add to the soup."

Lark wrinkled her nose. "I think I'll pass." Reaching for a cutting board and a knife, she asked, "Can I help you with the cutting?"

"That would be nice." Fitzy handed her a bundle of carrots, then pulled two sharp knives from the block.

They worked in companionable silence for a bit. The sound of their knives slicing through the veggies and hitting the wooden cutting boards made a steady, pleasant rhythm.

When Fitzy finished the celery, she reached for an onion. Peeling away the papery skin, she raised an eyebrow at Lark. "So, missy, what's on your mind?"

"Huh?" Lark looked up from the carrots. "What makes you think something's on my mind?"

"Because," said Fitzy with a knowing air, "I'm not just the housekeeper around here. I'm also your friend."

Lark smiled. "True."

"And I know you well enough to tell when something's bothering you. So start talking!"

Sighing, Lark put down the knife and rested her chin in her hands. "I'm writing a new song and I'm stuck. I mean, I know what I *want* to say, I just don't know how to say it. I can't make it come together."

"Been there," said Fitzy with a sympathetic sigh. "Happens to me all the time with new recipes."

"I think it might be because I'm not focusing," Lark said, only just realizing it. "See, I do have something else on my mind. I can't decide what I want out of life. I know I want to make music, but I just don't know if I'll ever be truly comfortable performing in front of people."

Fitzy looked at Lark, an amused expression on her face. "Don't you think you've got some time before you have to make that kind of decision?" she said, using the back of her hand to swipe a stray curl from her forehead.

"I guess. But I wish I knew now. I wish I could be certain one way or the other."

"Certainty isn't all it's cracked up to be," said Fitzy gently. "Did I ever tell you that when I was your age, I wanted to be a pilot?"

Lark blinked, unsure she'd heard that correctly. "A pilot? You mean, like, in an airplane?"

"In a jet, to be precise. I had dreams of taking to the sky, flying away into the wild blue yonder." Fitzy shook her head and sighed. "I wanted to fly around the world."

"That's incredible!" said Lark, trying to imagine it: Fitzy . . . behind the vast controls of an enormous jumbo jet. Fitzy . . . the woman who could whip up a gourmet meal for twenty with her eyes closed but could never remember which buttons to push when making microwave popcorn. A pilot!

"Why didn't you do it?"

"Oh, there were lots of reasons," said Fitzy, with a dismissive wave. "One was that I also loved cooking, and as it happened, I was darn good at it."

"Heck, yeah!" Lark agreed, grinning. "Well, most of the time, when there aren't any lima beans involved."

Fitzy laughed. "The point is, when I was your age, it could have gone either way. I kept dreaming about flying, but went on perfecting my culinary skills, too."

"And?"

"And now, instead of coming in for a landing on a runway somewhere, I'm here making soup with you. See? Things work out the way they're supposed to. Believe me, honey, if you're destined to be a performer, that's what'll happen. And if you're meant to be a songwriter, that's what you'll be." She dumped the chopped onions into a pan, plucked another from the pile, and smiled. "Maybe if you stop worrying about what you want from life, you'll find out what life wants from you."

Lark knew it was good advice. So what if her videos were popular online? That didn't mean she had to decide anything right this minute. She could simply sit back and enjoy knowing that people liked her music. In fact, right now the only decision she had to make was whether to move on to chopping the tomatoes or the zucchini.

She was just reaching for a plump red tomato when the doorbell rang.

＊

Lark eyed the stranger on the front porch—he was in his mid-thirties, she guessed, and dressed in an expensive-looking suit. His long hair was streaked with professional highlights, and he had a pair of trendy black-framed eyeglasses perched on the bridge of his nose. He was holding a tablet and looked from Lark to the screen, then back to Lark.

"Can I help you?" she asked warily.

The stranger smiled winningly. "I hope so. I've had a heck of a time tracking you down . . . Songbird."

"What did you just call me?"

The man turned the tablet around so she could see the screen, which was showing the video of "Everything's Working Out." "Songbird," he repeated. "That is what you call yourself, isn't it?"

Lark's heart thudded in her chest. The idea of being "tracked down" by a grown man she'd never met made her very uncomfortable. She stepped back, ready to slam the door in his face, but the man quickly held out a business card.

"I'm Daniel Baylor," he said. "CEO of Zeitgeist Records."

Lark stared at the card until the man slipped it back into his pocket.

"Look, Miss Campbell . . ." He smiled at the shocked expression on her face. "Yes, I know your real name."

"How?"

"I saw you on *Rise and Shine* this week. I tuned in to see the Abbey Road interview—I like to keep tabs on the competition, you see. Imagine my surprise when I discovered that Abbey Road was living with the talented young country singer I'd been searching for ever since I'd seen her YouTube video." He shook his head and laughed. "Talk about a small world, huh? After the interview, I did a little digging. Bridget had introduced you as Lark Campbell, and since I knew the boys were signed with Lotus Records, and that Lotus is owned by Donna Campbell, it all fell into place. Then it was just a matter of looking up Donna's home address, and here I am."

"But why?" asked Lark, still feeling cold in her belly.

"To offer you a record deal, of course. Frankly, I'm not sure why your mother hasn't signed you herself. But hey, Lotus's loss is Zeitgeist's gain, right?"

"Not necessarily," said Lark.

"Listen, let's cut right to the chase, shall we?" Daniel

Baylor tucked the tablet under his arm and began to gesture exuberantly with his hands. "I am prepared to offer you more money than you've ever dreamed of. Zeitgeist has three times the budget Lotus does. I can have you in the studio by the end of the month. In addition, I'll get you on all the major talk shows, and on the cover of every magazine you can name. With that fabulous voice, and wholesome, girl-next-door image, you'll take America by storm."

Lark was speechless. She was glad when she heard the familiar clicking of high heels on marble tile.

"What's going on here?" Donna demanded, striding purposefully across the foyer floor and placing herself between Lark and Daniel Baylor. "Did I just hear you offering my daughter a recording contract?"

Daniel gave her a smug look. "You did."

"Are you out of your mind?" Donna's voice rose to an angry roar. "She's twelve years old! She's not even allowed to ride her bike in the street without my permission, let alone sign a legal and binding business document!"

"I understand that," said Daniel calmly. "Naturally I wouldn't have expected her to sign anything without parental consent."

"And what makes you think I'd ever consent to Lark signing with a rival record company instead of my own?" Donna seethed.

Daniel casually examined his fingernails and shrugged.

"I just assumed there was a reason you hadn't offered her a contract."

"Such as?"

"Maybe Lotus isn't interested in developing country artists."

"Nice try, pal," said Donna, folding her arms across her chest. "Everyone in the music business knows that Holly Rose, who happens to be the biggest female star in country music right now, is a Lotus artist."

"Oh, that's right." Daniel gave her an icy smile. "I guess it slipped my mind. But as long as we've started a dialogue here, and since you haven't signed Songbird to Lotus—"

"*You* do not get to call her Songbird," Donna ground out through her teeth. "And the answer is no! Lark is not in the market for a recording contract."

Daniel's eyes flashed angrily. "From one record executive to another, let me ask you a question: Why would you go to all the trouble to import an act from Britain, when you've got a superstar right under your nose?" He smirked. "Could it be that maybe you just don't know real talent when you see it?"

It was at that moment that Fitzy appeared from the kitchen, carrying the giant knife she'd been using to chop vegetables. "Is there a problem, Mrs. Campbell?" she asked, glaring at the man on the porch, while giving the knife a menacing twirl.

Daniel got the message. Without another word, he turned and hurried off the porch, then hopped into his sports car and sped down the driveway.

Satisfied, Fitzy went back to the kitchen.

Lark would have liked to vanish, too, but she only managed to get two steps away from the door before her mother caught her arm.

"I knew you were angry about what Bridget pulled in the interview," said Donna in a trembling voice. "But I never thought you'd try to get even by humiliating me."

Lark was stunned. "Humiliating you?"

"What else would you call going behind my back and reaching out to a competitor to secure a recording contract?"

"I didn't do that!"

"Didn't you?" Donna's face was tight with fury—or maybe it was hurt. "Then explain to me how that smarmy creep knows you can sing."

Lark opened her mouth, then immediately closed it. It was time to come clean about the Songbird videos. She dug into her pocket, pulled out her phone, and found the Songbird posts on YouTube.

"Remember the video I showed you of me singing 'Homesick'?" she said. "When Aidan tried to pass it off as a song he wrote?"

"Of course I remember!"

"Well . . ." Lark held out the phone to Donna. "Mimi was supposed to take the video down after I proved that Aidan was a liar, but she forgot. And then it got popular. So she made another one for my new song. And now they're both getting lots of hits."

She checked the number and felt a little jolt when she saw that it was up to 127,000. *At least I'm keeping my promise to Mimi*, she thought gloomily.

"Daniel Baylor saw the videos," Lark went on. "He left a comment asking me to contact him, but I didn't! I swear! Then Bridget what's-her-name went and made a big deal about me in the TV interview, and he recognized me. That's how he figured out where to find me."

Lark held her mother's gaze for the space of a heartbeat, then looked away and shrugged.

The next sound she heard was the purposeful tapping of high heels on marble . . . but this time the sound was followed by the equally purposeful slamming of Donna's office door.

CHAPTER ELEVEN

The next morning Lark stayed in her room as long as she could, struggling with her new song, "Holding My Hand."

She told herself she wouldn't quit until she'd written at least one good verse.

After an hour of staring at a blank journal page, with her fingers motionless on her guitar strings, she renegotiated: she wouldn't quit until she'd written one good *line*.

As the minutes ticked silently by, she realized she'd settle for one *word* . . . and it didn't have to be any good!

But she couldn't even manage that.

Finally, she put her guitar aside and skulked downstairs. She found her mother seated at the kitchen table, sipping coffee.

And wearing hiking clothes. Shorts, camp shirt, boots . . . Lark could even smell the sunscreen.

She took this for exactly what it was—an apology—and gave her mother a hug.

"Oh, honey," said Donna, her eyes moist. "I'm so sorry I behaved the way I did. Of course I know you didn't call that imbecile from Poltergeist Records."

Lark laughed. "Zeitgeist. Although the whole thing *was* kind of spooky."

"I should have never exploded at you like that. I guess I just had a moment of insecurity. I had no right to question your loyalty to me, but I was afraid you agreed with that creep."

"Agreed with him about what?"

"About me not recognizing my own daughter's talent."

"How could I ever think that," said Lark, "when you're paying me to write the band's next single? And Mom—"

"Stop. Don't say another word." Donna held up her hand and sniffled. "Just go back upstairs and change into your hiking clothes. Save this conversation for the great outdoors."

Lark grabbed a blueberry muffin from a plate on the table and ran back to her room, smiling the entire way.

※

Two hours later, she and her mother were at the top of Mount Lee, overlooking the city and the iconic Hollywood sign. To Lark's disappointment, both were slightly obscured by the presence of a tall chain-link fence.

"Safety first, I guess," said Lark, pressing her eye to the fence and peeking through one of the diamond-shaped holes for a better look.

"More like 'vandalism prevention' first," said Donna. Then she frowned. "That was cynical, wasn't it? Maybe I've been in LA too long."

Lark wasn't so sure about that; she guessed there were plenty of cynics in Nashville, too.

"All right then," said Donna, taking a long sip from her water bottle. "Here's what I want to say. I hope you don't think for one second that I'm unaware of how talented you are. I might even go so far as to start throwing the word 'prodigy' around."

"Thank you," said Lark, allowing the warmth of the words to settle on her like the California sunshine.

"I love that you've found the courage to perform in front of an audience. And I can't even believe how lucky I am to have you writing songs for the band."

"If you ask me," said Lark. "I'm the lucky one. I mean, how many twelve-year-olds can say they've heard their original songs on the radio?"

"Right!" Donna smiled proudly. "And that's kind of the point. You're twelve years old. Not a baby anymore, I know, but not an adult yet, either. I don't want to rob you of your childhood by asking you to embark on a full-fledged singing career. Writing songs snuggled up on your bed in your pajamas is one thing, but recording and touring and being famous is something else altogether. You see how crazy it is for the boys."

Lark thought of Teddy and all the pressure he was under—struggling to keep up with his schoolwork, wondering if he'd get to play soccer again, and dealing with fans in study hall. It was far from having a normal life.

Then again, normal was just another word for average. And who ever aspired to being average? Teddy himself had said that being in the band was a great opportunity, even with all the stress.

It was so complicated. In a good way, but still . . . complicated.

"If and when the day comes that you decide you're ready to try life in the spotlight," Donna continued, her voice solemn as she reached out to sweep a lock of auburn hair from Lark's cheek, "I'll support you one hundred percent. That's a promise. Naturally, you'll join me at Lotus."

"Naturally," said Lark with a grin. "After all, it is the family business."

"There's more to it than that," said Donna, still serious. "I'd want you to sign with me so I can take care of you. Guide you in making good choices. Protect you. Like I'm looking after Ollie, Max, and Teddy. This is a hard business for kids. You know all the horror stories. I would never want you or Abbey Road to end up like some of those poor young stars who took the wrong path because no one was looking out for them."

"I won't," Lark assured her. "The boys won't either."

"I want you to look at that Hollywood sign and tell me what you see."

Once again Lark peered through the chain-link fence at the towering white letters propped on the hillside. From this angle, she could see how flat and narrow they were, not to mention the unsightly grid of metal work that held them upright. Not exactly a pretty sight.

"They look different close-up than they do from down below in the city," she said thoughtfully. "From far away they look impressive. But up close you can see that they're pretty insubstantial."

"Exactly," said Donna. "And as a girl who got an A on her last creative writing assignment, you'll understand what I mean when I say that your observation is an extremely accurate metaphor for stardom. Like this hike we just took, fame is truly an uphill climb. And when you get to the top, you might discover that it's a lot less impressive than it first appeared."

Lark considered this. "So are you saying you *don't* want me to pursue a career in music?"

"Nope." Donna shook her head. "I'm just saying I want you to look at the issue from all possible angles and take your time. You don't have to decide anything now."

"That's what Fitzy said. She told me to stop worrying

about what I want from life for a while and wait to see if I can figure out what life wants from me."

"Sage advice," said Donna with a nod. "Fitzy is a treasure, isn't she? Well, as long as we keep her away from the lima beans, that is."

Lark laughed.

They took another few moments to admire the breathtaking views of Los Angeles, then headed back down the trail.

"But there is one decision I feel qualified to make right now," Lark said as they walked.

"What's that?"

"I've decided that I'd like to spend my February vacation in Nashville."

Donna smiled. "Somehow that doesn't surprise me."

"I've been working on the new song you asked me to write, and I've been having some trouble with it. I think being back in the place where I first fell in love with music might help to clear out the cobwebs so I can write something great."

"Sounds like a wonderful plan," said Donna. "In fact, I'd go with you if I could. Holly Rose is appearing at the Grand Ole Opry that week and as the owner of her record label, not to mention her longtime friend, I'd love to be there."

"Why can't you?"

When Donna raised her eyebrows and looked at her quizzically, Lark laughed.

"Oh, right!" she said, unable to believe it had actually slipped her mind. "Abbey Road's album is being released the following week!"

Donna nodded. "I really need to be here in town to oversee the craziness leading up to the release. There's planning the launch party, finalizing the details of the tour, and God only knows what else. I explained it all to Holly. She understands."

"Can Daddy and I go see Holly at the Opry?" Lark asked.

"I'll set it up," said Donna, nodding. "It'll be nice for Holly to have old friends in the audience."

"Awesome!" A thrill shot through Lark as she imagined herself in the audience, seeing her former babysitter on the legendary stage where all the greats of country music had played. It wouldn't be Lark's first visit to the world-famous Grand Ole Opry, but it would be her first time seeing a performer she actually knew personally.

"You can call Daddy and let him know your plans as soon as we get home," said Donna, her expression clouding. "Unfortunately, I'll be dealing with the 'I Wonder' video."

"Dealing with it? What do you mean?"

"It's a train wreck," Donna said glumly. "Nobody on the team is happy with it at all. We may have to reshoot the whole thing. Although if the director didn't get it right the first time, I don't know why he'd be any better the second time around. Maybe we need a fresh pair of eyes."

Lark stopped walking. "Mimi!"

"What about Mimi?" Donna asked, halting in her tracks.

"Mimi can be your fresh eyes! Let her direct the reshoot. Or at least contribute. She's got a lot of cool footage from the day we went shopping with the boys, and she's a genius at editing."

Donna looked skeptical. "I don't know, honey. Mimi doesn't have any real experience."

"She has plenty of experience," Lark countered. "The videos she made for my songs are amazing. Just let her show you the mall footage, and maybe brainstorm a few ideas for fixing the 'I Wonder' video. Please!"

"Well," said Donna, grinning, "it wouldn't be the first time a friend of yours stepped in to save Abbey Road. Teddy was a godsend. Maybe Mimi will prove to be the same."

Lark didn't doubt it for a minute.

CHAPTER TWELVE

The following Friday morning as Lark waited for the school bus, she reflected on all that had happened since her hike with Donna to the Hollywood sign—a mere five days ago.

Mimi had thoroughly impressed everyone with her footage of the impromptu concert at the mall. She'd been brought in as a "media intern" to help with conceptualizing, producing, and editing the "I Wonder" video.

Lark was proud of her, but if she were going to be honest, she was also the tiniest bit jealous. Mimi, in her capacity as intern, had been spending most of her after-school free time working with the director, the lighting crew, Jas (the choreographer), and of course, Abbey Road. Ordinarily, Mimi would have been hanging out with Lark.

Lark missed Mimi. It wasn't that she didn't want "I

Wonder" to be a huge success; she just wanted a little best-friend time, too.

But it couldn't be helped. The video had already been delayed, so things had to move quickly. Mimi was going on a ski vacation to Colorado with her family next week and Donna wanted the editing completed before she left.

Which was why Lark did not want to miss the bus this morning. She was leaving for Nashville the next day and this would be her last chance to spend time with Mimi for a whole week.

❋

Mimi had saved Lark their usual seat, but it wasn't until Lark was halfway down the bus aisle that she realized Mimi was sound asleep! She noted the dark circles under her friend's eyes, and understood that all the late nights Mimi had put in on the video had really taken their toll on the budding filmmaker.

Slipping quietly into the seat beside Mimi, Lark took out her songwriting journal and tinkered with the chorus of "Holding My Hand." But when the bus driver took a tight corner a little too quickly, she went sliding across the seat and crashed into Mimi, who awoke with a start.

"Huh? What? W-where are we?" Mimi sputtered groggily.

"Almost at school," Lark reported. "I didn't want to wake you up. You look tuckered out."

"If that means exhausted beyond belief, then that's exactly what I am," Mimi said through a yawn. "I was up most of the night editing the footage we shot yesterday. But I'm happy to say it looks great. Hey, have I thanked you for recommending me for this job?"

Lark giggled. "Only about twenty trillion times."

"Well, let's make it twenty trillion and one." Mimi threw her arms around Lark and gave her a grateful squeeze. "Thank you again. This has been the most exciting and interesting week of my life!"

"Thank *you*," said Lark. "You're doing my mom a huge favor helping out like this."

Now Mimi eyed the journal on Lark's lap. "How's the new song coming along?"

"Slowly," Lark admitted.

"You'll get there," Mimi told her. "You always do. And going to Nashville is going to be a huge help."

"That's what I'm hoping," said Lark, slipping the journal back into her backpack as the bus pulled into the school drive.

✳

Lark didn't run into Teddy until fourth period, when they were both heading toward the science corridor. He looked extremely stressed.

"What's wrong?" she asked, giving him a sympathetic smile. "Aren't you excited for February vacation?"

"Yeah, totally," he said. "It's just that there were a bunch of paparazzi outside my house this morning. One of them snapped a photo of my mom when she went out to get the newspaper. Her hair was a mess and she was wearing her old bathrobe. Trust me, she was *not* happy."

"I don't blame her," said Lark.

Teddy managed a smile. "I'm sorry to be such a downer. I know I should be on top of the world right now, with school break, and then the album launch after that. I think I'll be a lot more relaxed after I get through my science exam. It's this period. I just hope I don't find a photographer hiding under the lab table."

Lark laughed. "If you did, it would be almost as weird as what happened to me last weekend." Then, in an effort to make him feel less self-conscious about finding photographers camped in his yard, she proceeded to tell him all about the pushy music executive from Zeitgeist arriving on her doorstep and offering her a recording deal.

"The guy actually came to your house, rang your doorbell, and offered you a contract?" Teddy said, shaking his head in disbelief.

"Creepy, huh?"

"A little, I guess. But also pretty darn cool."

Lark gave him an astonished look. "Cool? How is that cool?"

"Granted, this Baylor dude's tactics were kind of aggressive," said Teddy. "And I don't blame you for feeling uncomfortable about it. But think about it—there are people who spend their whole lives dreaming about getting that kind of break. Most musicians struggle for years, trying to connect with a manager or a producer or a record label, and it never happens. But you've got people literally knocking down your door."

"I guess it was kind of flattering," Lark admitted.

"There's just one thing I don't get," said Teddy as they arrived at door of his science classroom. "How did the guy find out about you?"

Lark's heart sank. She'd totally forgotten that Teddy didn't know anything about Songbird's YouTube presence.

Thankfully, she was spared answering his question by the third-period bell.

"Oh, gosh . . . there's the bell . . . gonna be late for English," she stammered. "Good luck on that science test. I know you're gonna crush it!"

"Wait . . . ," said Teddy. "How did he know?"

But Lark was already halfway down the hall.

❋

"Songwriting journal?"

"In my carry-on."

"Computer and cell-phone chargers?"

"In my suitcase."

"Did you remember to pack your toothbrush?"

Lark rolled her eyes. "Yes, Mom, I packed my toothbrush. And even if I didn't, I'm sure Daddy would buy me one in Nashville."

"You're right," said Donna with a nervous sigh. "Of course you're right. I'm just feeling a little antsy, I guess. I hate the thought of you being away for a whole week."

As they made their way through the airport, Lark shook off the embarrassing memory of fainting in the baggage claim the day Ollie and Max had first arrived from London. The security guard had thought it was Ollie's smile that had caused her to swoon, but really, it was because her mother had asked her to sing in public.

It was hard to believe, since she was now actually entertaining the idea of becoming a performer.

"Are you going to ask Daddy for input on the new song?" Donna asked as they hurried through the departures terminal.

"Definitely," said Lark.

"Good. And have him take you shopping for something cute to wear to the Opry. Or maybe Holly has something you can borrow. You did pack your cowboy boots, didn't you?"

"Nope."

Donna looked stricken. "Why not?"

"'Cause I'm wearing them, Mama, that's why!"

When they arrived at the security checkpoint, Donna pulled Lark close and gave her a powerful hug. "Safe trip, darling. You be a good girl, hear? And you make sure Daddy takes you to our favorite restaurant!"

"Martin's Bar-B-Que Joint," said Lark, her mouth watering just thinking about it.

"That's right. Have some ribs for me."

"Half slab?" Lark asked, grinning.

"Well, since I won't actually be eating them, make it a full slab," said Donna. "As they say at Martin's, you might as well go 'whole hog'!"

Lark had every intention of doing just that.

CHAPTER
THIRTEEN

"Songbird!" Jackson Campbell's voice rang through the arrivals terminal at Nashville International Airport.

Lark ran straight for him through the crowd. He caught her and swung her up into a hug, kissing her cheeks and nearly squeezing the breath out of her.

"Welcome home, darlin'."

"Thanks, Daddy. It feels good to be back."

As they followed the stream of travelers toward the baggage claim, Jackson reached into his pocket and pulled out an envelope.

"What's that?"

"A little something Garret Givens asked me to pass along," said Jackson vaguely. "Go ahead, open it."

Lark tore into the envelope and gasped at what she saw: a check! For a lot of money.

"That's a whole bunch of zeroes, isn't it?" she said.

"It's payment for the lyrics for 'Divorce Hurts.' They think it's gonna be a huge hit!"

"Wow," said Lark, still gaping at the number.

"Any ideas about what you'd like to spend it on?" asked Jackson.

"Actually, I know exactly what I want to spend it on. I'll have to make a few phone calls, but I think I have just enough time to make it happen."

When Lark told Jackson her plan, he agreed that it was an excellent idea. Then she gave him a quick rundown of what was going on in her life, starting with her writer's block.

"It's so frustrating," she grumbled as they positioned themselves beside the conveyor belt. "I know the song is in there somewhere, I just can't get at it."

"That's not such an unusual situation," Jackson assured her. "It happens to all songwriters now and then. You just need to set the song aside for a while. Leave it be, let it rest. A song is like a doe in the forest. If you go chasing after it, you'll never catch it. You've just got to relax and be still, and let it come to you."

"Okay," said Lark. "That's what I'll do, I'll relax. Oh! There's my suitcase."

Jackson collected her luggage and they were on their way.

✳

Dear Mom,

Miss you! Dad surprised me by inviting
Brandi and Kayla over to the house for a
sleepover (Remember them? We were really
close in fifth grade!). It was so much fun.
We compared notes on middle school in
Nashville vs. LA. The verdict: middle school
is torture no matter where you live! I want to
invite them to visit us in Cali, okay? Tonight
we're meeting up with Aunt Delilah and Uncle
Bobby for dinner at Martin's Bar-B-Que!
Daddy's already talking about the Catfish
Redneck Tacos he's gonna order! Hope things
are going well with the album launch. Don't
work too hard.
Love, Lark

✻

Hey Mimi,

OMG Nashville is just what I needed to clear
my head! Daddy and me went camping for a
night in the Smoky Mountains. We brought
our guitars and played under the moon.
You would love the light and the scenery
there. You'll have to come with me sometime.
Imagine the videos you could shoot! Speaking

of videos, I told MY daddy all about Songbird
being such a big hit on YouTube and he was
super proud . . . of me AND YOU, for having
such great artistic vision. Hope YOU're having
fun on the slopes. Miss U tons!!!
XO
—L
P.S. How's Trevor Yoshida? Wink, wink!

＊

Hey Max!
Hope you guys aren't using up all MY good
shampoo! How's superstardom treating YOU?!
Mimi texted me that everybody in Colorado
is talking about the upcoming Abbey Road
album. Congrats! You really need to come to
Nashville ASAP. Music is everywhere! You
can smell it in the air and taste it in the
water. At night, before I go to bed I have to
shake the music out of MY hair. You guys
would love it here. The whole city hums. Best
news EVER: tonight Daddy and me are going
to see Holly Rose at the Grand Ole Opry
(remember the night she jammed with Y'all
in the backyard and Aidan tried to flirt with
her? Ha ha). We're going to visit her in her

dressing room before the show. I bet she's
nervous, but who wouldn't be? (Probably
Ollie!) I would faint dead away if I ever set
foot onstage at the Opry. Believe it or not,
I miss you guys! Looking forward to your
album launch party the day I get back!
See you soon,
Lark
P.S. Tell Teddy I say hey.
P.P.S. No, don't tell him.
P.P.P.S Okay, tell him, but don't make a thing
of it.

Lark had been to the Opry before, but never backstage.
Tonight she was going to experience the kind of magic
known only to the biggest stars of country music.

"C'mon, Daddy," she urged, bouncing up and down in
the passenger seat of her father's pickup. "Can't you drive a
little bit faster?"

"Not unless I want to get a speeding ticket." Jackson
chuckled. "Be patient. We're almost there. How about a pop
quiz to pass the time?"

"Pop quiz?" Lark frowned. "Daddy, I'm off from school
this week! Last thing I want to do is take a quiz."

"I think you'll enjoy this one," said Jackson. "Okay, darlin', true or false: the Grand Ole Opry show began as a television variety show."

"False," said Lark. "It was a radio broadcast called the WSN Barn Dance. WSM AM still broadcasts live from the Opry."

Jackson let out a long whistle. "Dang, girl. You really know your stuff! So how about you give me a question?"

"Okay." Lark thought for a minute. "Here's one. When they built the new Opry House way back in 1974, what did they bring along with them from the original Ryman Auditorium?"

"You mean besides some of the greatest country stars of all time?"

"Yes, besides that."

Jackson furrowed his brow and pretended to be stumped. "Gee, Songbird, I don't know. Can you give me a hint?"

"Daddy! I know you know this one!"

"Hmmm ... could it be ... a six-foot circle of hard-wood flooring cut from the original stage, which was placed dead center in the new stage, so performers can stand on a little piece of Opry history?"

"That would be absolutely right!"

"Of course it's right. And do you know what else?"

"What?"

"We're here!"

Lark let out a squeak of delight as Jackson pulled into a parking space.

"Let's go!" she cried, leaping out of the truck's cab like a jackrabbit. "Holly's waiting!"

✳

She was waiting in the Women of Country dressing room, to be precise.

"This is it!" Lark knocked.

"Come on in!"

She opened the door and there was Holly, looking stunning in a long sequined green dress that reminded Lark of mermaid scales. On her feet were a pair of battered cowboy boots. Lark ran over and gave her a hug.

"I'm so glad y'all could make it," said Holly, in her rich, melodic voice.

"Wouldn't miss it for the world," said Jackson, leaning down to place a fatherly kiss on top of Holly's blond head.

"Let me look at you, little one!" Holly held Lark at arm's length and studied her with big, brown eyes. "You're gorgeous!"

"Hope my outfit's all right," said Lark. She was wearing a denim jacket she'd pulled from the closet of her Tennessee bedroom over the sweet little dress she'd purchased that afternoon on a shopping trip with Aunt Delilah. Just like Holly, Lark had paired the dress with her old boots to achieve the perfect, breezy country girl look.

"It's fabulous" said Holly. "And your hair!"

"Y'all like it?" Lark's hand went to the long, loose side braid draped over her shoulder. "My friend Brandi did it for me."

"Give me her number," joked Holly. "I might be able to use her . . . if my hair ever grows in!"

She was referring to the fact that her once long corn silk–colored curls were now cropped into a cute little bob.

"I love your hair," said Lark. "It looks great on you."

"Thanks, but I miss my long hair." Holly rolled her eyes. "That'll teach me to listen to stylists instead of following my own instincts. And speaking of instincts, how's the song-writing going?"

"Unfortunately, our Songbird's in the throes of a nasty case of writer's block," Jackson explained. "I told her she'd get over it soon enough."

"Your daddy's right. Happens to all of us, but it passes." Holly's eyes sparkled as she leaned close Lark's ear. "By the way, I've heard music business people talking about a pretty little country singer who's becoming a YouTube sensation. They say she calls herself Songbird. I'm guessing it's you."

Lark bobbed her head, feeling an odd mixture of pride and embarrassment. "No need to whisper. Daddy knows all about it. So does Mama."

"Well, I can't tell you how happy I am to hear it, baby doll," said Holly. "You've got talent and it's time the whole world knew it. Because music, especially country music, exists for one reason—to make people happy! It puts them in touch with something deep and human and real they can't always find on their own. The best music makes people *feel*."

Again, Lark nodded. She believed what Holly was saying, every word, to the depths of her soul.

"It's a gift to be able to do that," Holly said. "And I'd hate to see your gift go to waste."

"I know. But I don't think I have the guts to be a star. All the attention, and the gossip and the expectations."

Holly laughed. "Let me ask you something. What was the last bit of gossip you heard about me?"

"Well . . . um . . ." Lark bit her lip, thinking. "I don't reckon I've heard any. I mean, there's always news, like about your songs being in the charts or your concerts being sold out. But never anything nasty or personal."

"That's right. Because I'm doing the fame thing on my own terms. I don't misbehave, I don't prance around in skimpy little outfits, and I don't pitch a hissy fit if someone brings me the wrong coffee order. I keep it all about the music. So that's what people focus on."

Jackson cleared his throat. "Hate to interrupt all this secret girl talk," he teased, "but Songbird, we'd best be on our way. Holly Rose has got a job to do. And we've got front-row seats."

Lark gave Holly another big hug. "Thanks," she said. "And knock 'em dead out there."

"I always do, darlin'," said Holly, snapping her a wink. "I always do!"

＊

Holly Rose's set was amazing! She sang all her current hits, and even a couple of crowd-pleasing classics—"Here You Come Again," by Dolly Parton, and "I Fall to Pieces," by Patsy Cline.

"Thank you, everybody!" came Holly's voice over the thunder of cheers and applause. "Gosh, it is just so exciting for me to be here! I've got one more song to perform for y'all tonight. And because the Opry is all about being part of a family, I'm going to invite a couple of very special people who really are like family to come on up here and join me onstage." Shading her eyes against the glare of the spotlight, she scanned the front row. "Jackson, Lark, where are y'all?!"

Lark's eyes flew wide open.

Jackson was already on his feet, extending his hand to his little girl. "Let's go, darlin'."

"No!" Lark shook her head hard. "Daddy, no! I can't!"

"Sure you can!"

"But . . . but . . . it's the *Grand Ole Opry*!"

"All the more reason," said Jackson, laughing as he pulled her gently to her feet.

"What if I faint?"

"Then I'll catch ya." He was guiding her toward the steps at the front of the stage.

"What if I'm off-key?"

"Not gonna happen."

"Daddy, I'm scared. I'm shaking."

"I know, darlin'. 'Cause that's what people do before the greatest moments of their lives. Holly wants us to share her big night. We can't very well say no, can we?"

"I guess not," Lark murmured, trembling as the soles of her boots hit the hardwood of the legendary stage.

"Ladies and gentlemen," said Holly, "please join me in welcoming my dear friends the Campbells. This is Jackson—"

Jackson waved to the cheering crowd with one hand, while holding Lark steady with the other.

"And this here is his little girl," Holly went on, reaching out to take Lark's hand and draw her into the circle made of pale wooden floorboards. "Her name's Lark—and she's a real little songbird."

The minute Lark heard Holly strum the acoustic intro, she knew exactly what song they were going to sing. It was one Holly had sang for Lark, Donna, and Jackson in their Tennessee backyard on a starry night. The first song she'd ever written, it was called "Reaching," and both Lark and Jackson knew it by heart.

Reaching higher than the moon,
I know it's gonna happen soon.
And on some country night like this,
I'll reach for the stars and I won't miss.

The voices of the three old friends melted together like butter on a biscuit. When Holly stepped back from the mic to let Lark sing the second verse solo, the music came from somewhere deep within her. From some secret spot that was part of her soul. And with it came the courage.

When the song finished, Lark felt a rush of pride and joy. The crowd was on their feet, whooping and whistling.

"That's for us," Lark breathed, astonished.

"No, darlin'," Holly whispered in her ear. "That's for *you*." Then she stepped up to the mic and said, "You saw her here first, folks. Lark Campbell, Nashville's little songbird! And something tells me this ain't the last time she'll be gracing this stage!"

Judging by the reaction of the crowd, they were in complete agreement.

Much later that night, as the moon spilled silver ribbons through Lark's bedroom window, she slipped out of bed and picked up her guitar.

Opening her songwriting journal, she turned to the page labeled "Holding My Hand." Reading what she'd written on the page, she hummed the melody and strummed a few chords.

Nothing wrong with the tune, she thought, smiling. Then she reached for a pencil and made a small but significant change to the title.

Holding My ~~Hand~~ Own

It was as if she'd just struck musical oil! The lyrics came in a gush, and the notes were like sparks shooting between her fingertips and the guitar strings. Her voice brought them together:

Whatever fate has got in store,
This girl ain't afraid no more.
It's time to face the great unknown,
And you can bet I'll hold my own.

Lark heard clapping and looked to see her father leaning in the doorway.

"Looks like you got over your writer's block," he said softly.

Lark sighed. "Standing in that circle tonight, holding my own on the most famous stage in country music and getting a standing ovation . . ." She shook her head in amazement. "It was like I was a part of something way bigger than myself."

"I get that," said Jackson, coming to stand beside her bed and ruffle her hair. "After all, when you stepped into that circle, you were literally walking in the footsteps of all your musical idols. You were standing where your heroes stood before you."

"I guess so. But you know what, Daddy?"

"What's that, Songbird?"

She smiled up at him through the moonlight. "My biggest hero is standing right here."

✳

Lark bounded off the plane and ran all the way down the jet bridge. She couldn't wait to tell her mother about her night onstage at the Opry, and what she had decided in its wake.

The ride from her daddy's house to Nashville International had been bittersweet and tearful, but once the plane had taken off, Lark was surprised to discover just how excited she was to be going back to LA. After all, in addition to her mother, Mimi, and the boys, there was a future in show business to look forward to now.

"Lark!" cried Donna, waving from the gate.

"Mom!"

"It's so great to have you home, baby. We've missed you so much!"

"Missed you too!" She felt a twinge of disappointment that the boys weren't there to greet her; she hadn't expected Teddy, but she was a bit surprised that Max and Ollie hadn't come along. Donna explained that they had a dance session with Jas and couldn't cancel it.

They made quick work of retrieving her luggage and getting to the car. Once they were on the highway, Lark turned to Donna in the driver's seat and said, with absolute certainty, "Mama, I want to make music!"

Donna gave her a sideways look. "Are we talking professionally?"

"Yes, ma'am," said Lark with an emphatic nod. "No more hiding in the wings or keeping to the shadows. I want to perform! Live! And record, and write my own songs, and make music videos."

There was a brief moment of silence, then Donna let out an enthusiastic "Yeeeee haw!" that seemed to come up from the tips of her toes.

"Careful, Mom," said Lark, giggling, "Your Nashville is showing!"

"I can't help it! Oh, Lark, I am so happy!"

"Me too. But there's more."

"Okay . . ."

Lark couldn't think of a better way to explain her feelings about pursuing a career in music than by showing her mother the lyrics to the song she'd written the night before. So she waited until the SUV was stopped at a traffic light, then opened her journal to the page and handed it to Donna to read.

I'm gonna choose what works for me,
And become the star I want to be.
With your love, I'll never be alone,
But now it's time for me to hold my own.

When Donna finished reading, her eyes were filled with tears.

"Oh, Mama, if I'm going to sign with Lotus, you can't just start bawling every time I sing a song. If you do, you'll end up dehydrated!"

"I know, I know," said Donna, laughing as she wiped her cheeks. "It's just that you're so talented. That song is beautiful, and your voice is amazing. And most of all, you're such a great kid!"

"That's exactly what I want everyone to remember," said Lark, her tone serious. "I'm a kid. I don't want anything to happen overnight. I want to take my time and do it on my own terms. Okay?"

"Definitely," said Donna, hitting the turn signal and

guiding the car onto their street. "In which case, you should sign what's called an artist development deal."

Lark raised an eyebrow. "Development? Does this have anything to do with me wearing a training bra?"

Donna laughed. "No, honey. An artist development deal allows you to move at your own pace. No crazy deadlines, no exhausting schedules. It's the best way to nurture a young artist. You'll have the chance to move at your own speed and learn from older artists, like Holly. Local gigs only, no national tours."

"So I don't have to take a leave of absence like Teddy? I can stay in school?"

"Of course. Teddy's career is already in motion, and he has an obligation to his bandmates. He inherited the velocity of Abbey Road when he joined. But you'll have the luxury of going at your own pace. And as a solo act, you only have to answer to yourself." Donna gave her a sly grin. "And me."

Lark smiled. She wondered if it was weird that a twelve-year-old girl actually *wanted* to go to school; she suspected most kids would welcome the chance to put lockers and lunchrooms behind them in exchange for a whirlwind concert tour.

But Lark Campbell was not most kids.

"That song, 'Holding My Own' . . . ," said Donna. "It sounds suspiciously like the track you were writing for Abbey Road before you left." She shot Lark a grin.

"You're right," said Lark. "It was originally called 'Holding My Hand.' But don't worry, I'm not going to let you down. In fact, I already started writing a new song on the plane. It will be perfect for Abbey Road's next album."

"What's it called?" asked Donna.

Lark smiled as Donna guided the car toward the driveway. "It's called 'Right Back Where I Wanna Be,'" she said. "And I think you'll love it."

✳

To Lark's surprise, there was a crowd gathered in the street where their driveway met the road.

"This is new," Lark observed.

"Well, a lot can happen in a week." Donna carefully maneuvered the SUV around the strangers loitering by the driveway's entrance. "The boys did tons of media while you were gone, and there's a really great buzz about the album."

Lark nodded. "Daddy and I saw a few of their appearances. They were great on *Entertainment Access*. Ollie was so funny."

"He always is," said Donna with a grin. "But in retrospect, it probably wasn't the best idea to have you return on album launch day. We've got a lot to do before the party tonight. And the tour is only a couple of weeks away!"

Lark frowned as a photographer tossed a gum wrapper into the azaleas Fitzy had planted around the mailbox. "Isn't this illegal?"

"It would be," said Donna, "if they were actually on our property. Technically, it's not trespassing if they stay in the street."

Girls were holding signs that said I LOVE YOU OLLIE and TEDDY 4-EVER. One girl wore a sweatshirt on which she'd airbrushed the words MARRY ME MAX.

"Hope this doesn't change your mind about a music career," said Donna, sounding as if she were only half teasing.

"What would be the point?" said Lark. "If I'm dealing with crazy fans outside my house anyway, a few of them might as well be there for me." She laughed, but in truth she wondered how it would feel to have people loitering outside her house carrying signs with her name on them. Would it be exciting? Or scary?

She guessed it would probably be a little of both, and she'd just have to figure it out as she went along.

Inside, Max and Ollie greeted her with hugs. Teddy hung back and waved, but he was smiling ear to ear. Seeing him made Lark's heart skip a beat; she hadn't realized how much she missed him, and it was clear that he'd missed her, too.

"Welcome home, Lark," said Max. "How was the trip?"

"Great!" said Lark. "And I actually have some news . . ."

"So do we," said Ollie. "Julia just called. *British Invasion*'s only been officially released for a few hours and it's already gone to number one on the iTunes chart!"

CHAPTER FOURTEEN

After a lightning round of congratulatory hugs and toasts of sparkling cider, Donna shifted into party-prep mode. She called Julia and started issuing reminders about the night's menu and double-checking the guest list, which read like a who's who of the music industry's power players.

The bash to celebrate the release of *British Invasion* would be taking place at a very trendy club called Dusk. Lark couldn't help but feel a bit of personal pride about the album's success. After all, two of the songs on it, "Homesick" and "Wounded Pride," were written by her.

Lark joined her mother and the boys in the kitchen, where Fitzy had set out a feast of snacks—chips and salsa with home-made guacamole, and a plate of chocolate-covered cherries.

"To album-release day!" said Ollie, raising a tortilla chip in a festive gesture.

"Here's to big sales and great reviews," Max chimed in, taking a cherry and clinking it against Ollie's chip.

"The minute this record goes platinum," said Ollie, his trademark confidence shining in his handsome face, "I'm going to buy myself a Maserati. No, make that a Ferrari. Or maybe a Jaguar—I'm a Brit after all."

"Why don't you just buy one of each?" Max suggested, dunking a chip into the spicy salsa.

"Excellent idea," said Ollie. "I think I will."

"That's awful big talk," Lark teased, "from a guy who doesn't even have his driver's license yet."

"Who said anything about driving?" Ollie shot back with a grin. "I'll just park them in the driveway and admire them."

"That'll certainly save petrol," Max observed.

"Not to mention lives," added Lark. "I'm going up to my room to unpack."

But that wasn't entirely true. Like her music mogul mother, Lark also had some calls to make regarding the launch party.

She had invited some very special guests, and she wanted to make sure they were ready for the big night.

❊

Lark couldn't believe that her mother was letting her wear mascara. *And* lip gloss—a shiny pinkish-peach with a hint of frost. Not only was the lip gloss the perfect complement to her hair and skin tone, it also went beautifully with her brand-new silvery-peach dress.

"You look very grown-up," said Donna, when Lark met her at the bottom of the stairs. "Glamorous, in fact."

"Thanks," said Lark. "You look glamorous, too."

"Why thank you," said Donna, smoothing her elegant lace skirt.

There was a commotion in the upstairs hall and Lark turned to see Max and Ollie roughhousing on their way toward the staircase.

"Don't you dare wrinkle those outfits!" Donna scolded.

"Sorry, we're just excited," said Max.

"And dashing!" Lark added. "For a couple of shampoo-stealing, cereal-hogging, loud-mouthed slobs, that is."

"Well, this slob thinks you look like a princess," said Ollie, rushing down the steps to give her a gallant bow.

"Perfection," Max agreed, tipping an imaginary hat as Lark spun around to show off her party dress.

"Teddy's meeting us there," said Donna, heading for the door. "So we should be getting on our way!"

"Wait," said Lark, scooping the keys to the SUV from the foyer table. "You forgot these."

"Actually, I won't be needing them tonight." Donna threw open the front door to reveal a black stretch limousine waiting in the driveway. "Surprise!"

Max's mouth fell open.

Ollie grinned. "Brilliant."

"I splurged," said Donna, shrugging. "I thought it was only fitting that the guests of honor arrive in style."

As Lark followed the boys out of the house and into the luxurious backseat of the elegant car, she felt a tumble of excitement in her chest. Because she, too, had arranged a special surprise.

And the sooner they got to the party, the sooner she could unveil it.

*

When the limo pulled up to Dusk, Lark was sure she'd arrived at some sort of mystical fairyland. The entire facade of the nightclub was bathed in a blue-and-lavender glow and dotted with glimmering points of light, which made it look as if an entire galaxy of stars had fallen from the heavens and landed in downtown Los Angeles.

Stylishly dressed guests waited in line while a man in a dark suit checked their invitations. The sight of the long, black vehicle gliding up to the curb made every head turn.

"I can't believe this is all for us," said Max in a hushed voice.

"Get used to it," Ollie advised, crooking a grin. "'Cause this is only the beginning!"

When the driver came around to open the car door, Lark could hear Abbey Road's "Dream of Me" blaring through the club's outdoor speakers. As the familiar melody flooded the cool night air, Lark felt a surge of pride for the two British boys she'd come to think of as her big brothers.

And, of course, for Teddy. Teddy, who was suddenly standing beside the driver, looking very grown-up in a blue blazer and extending his hand to help Lark out of the car.

Flashbulbs erupted around them like fireworks as she placed her fingertips in his.

"Sure beats gym class, huh?" he whispered in her ear.

Lark laughed. "You can say that again."

"Hey, Abbey Road!" a photographer shouted. "Get together, guys."

Teddy let go of Lark's hand and went to join his bandmates. Positioning themselves in front of the club's door, the three talented young men stood with their arms around each other's shoulders, smiling broadly.

Sliding her own arm around her mother's waist, Lark said, "This is amazing, Mom."

Donna nodded, nearly overcome with emotion. "It's exactly how I pictured it," she said. "All those months ago when I showed you that silly video. This is what I was hoping and praying and planning for."

"You're the one who made it happen," Lark reminded her. "This is your night as much as theirs."

"I couldn't have done it without you," Donna said, giving Lark a squeeze.

"Me? What'd I do?"

"You were patient with me, and let me follow my dream." When Lark raised a doubtful eyebrow, Donna laughed. "Okay, so maybe you weren't always patient, but that's understandable. You could have complained a lot more than you have. I mean, I did uproot you from your life in Nashville, and I'm hardly ever around." She paused to wipe a tear from her cheek. "And I know it hasn't been fun for you, living paycheck to paycheck—"

"Mama," said Lark, cutting her off. "It's all right. Honest."

"Hey, Lark!" Max was calling. "Donna! Come over here."

Donna and Lark exchanged excited smiles, then scampered over to join the group, beaming for the cameras.

It was a moment before Lark realized that she wasn't feeling at all self-conscious or afraid. Could it be that she was growing into the idea of fame?

Maybe I really could *get used to this,* she thought.

"Okay," said Donna, addressing the paparazzi, "time to get these superstars inside. There'll be plenty of time for photos later in the evening."

As they made their way through the velvet ropes, Lark caught up to Max.

"Thanks for including us in that picture," she said.

"Of course," said Max. "What kind of celebration would this be without a family photo or two?"

"Funny you should mention family . . . ," said Lark as

two dark-suited gentlemen opened Dusk's towering glass doors. She pointed straight ahead, where three smiling people were waiting in the club's vestibule.

Max stopped in his tracks, blinking as if he couldn't believe his eyes. "Mum? Dad? . . . *Anna!*"

A pretty girl with long, brown curls and enormous green eyes ran forward to fling herself into Max's arms. "Maxie!" she cried. "Surprise!"

Max held his sister tight and spun her around, laughing out loud. When Max had placed Anna gently back on her feet, his parents joined the gleeful family embrace.

"I can't believe you're here," said Max, his voice catching. "But how—?"

"Lark arranged it," said Anna. "She even paid for our airline tickets."

"And we couldn't be more grateful," said Max's mother in her musical Jamaican accent. "We wouldn't have missed this night for the world."

Max turned to Lark, looking overwhelmed. "I don't understand," he whispered. "I know money's been tight for you and Donna. How did you ever manage to afford three plane tickets from London?"

"I used the money I earned from the song I wrote for the Hatfields. Daddy gave me the check when I was in Nashville, and I called your folks and set it all up." She smiled at Anna, who was now looking around at the glittering nightclub with an expression of awe. "There's nothing I would have rather spent it on, Max. Like you said, it wouldn't have been much of a celebration without family."

❋

Not surprisingly, it didn't take Ollie long to get his flirt on. Within the first ten minutes of entering the club he was surrounded by a bevy of fashion models, pop singers, and waitresses. It seemed there wasn't a female alive who could resist Oliver Wesley's charms.

Lark and Anna, who were the same age, spent some time talking to the twin daughters of one of the album's producers, who were also in middle school. They were joined by Teddy and a boy named Devin, Julia the PR specialist's younger brother. Devin was a freshman at a private high school in Rancho Palos Verdes, and Anna developed an instant crush on him. They were the youngest guests at the party and none of them could get over the fact that they were at such a cool event—and at a real nightclub, no less!

Lark was delighted when Fitzy arrived on Jas's arm! She was dressed to the nines and looking sharp, even as she turned up her nose at some of the fancier hors d'oeuvres.

"Salmon mousse on cucumber slices?" she scoffed, waving away the waiter who offered the offending morsels on a silver tray. "Who in the world would ever come up with such a peculiar combination?"

Lark gaped at her. "Seriously, Fitz?" She laughed. "I can't believe you just said that!"

"What do you mean?" Fitzy asked innocently.

"I think," said Teddy, "she means bacon blondies, parsnip cookies, tuna fish and banana sandwiches . . ."

"It's called being innovative!" Fitzy huffed.

Because Dusk was one of the best dance clubs in the city, Donna had arranged for DJ Lucious to provide entertainment for the evening. Lark shrieked with laughter as Fitzy and Jas hit the dance floor.

"Who knew Fitzy could throw shapes like that?" said Teddy.

Without warning, Max snuck up behind Lark and whisked her onto the floor. "We can't let Fitzy show us up," he cried. "Come on, let's show her how it's done."

Lark realized that this was the first time she'd ever danced with a boy in public. She knew it would be good practice for the RRMS seventh-grade semiformal that would be held in the spring (assuming anyone asked her); nonetheless, dancing with someone as talented as Max was a bit intimidating.

Halfway through the song, she noticed Ollie waving Max over to the stage beside the DJ booth, where a microphone had been set up.

"What's that about?" Lark asked.

"Hey, you aren't the only one who can plan a surprise," said Max, winking. "The band's put together a little tribute."

"A tribute? To who?"

Max didn't answer, he just twirled her to the edge of the dance floor, where Donna was chatting with a fashion designer and a reality TV personality.

"What's going on?" Donna asked.

Max gave her a smile filled with mischief. "You'll see!" he said, then jogged over to where Teddy and Oliver were waiting.

"What have they got up their sleeves?" Donna asked.

Lark shrugged.

When the three band members had assembled, Max nodded to DJ Lucious, who cut the music. Ollie tapped on the mic to call for the crowd's attention.

"Thank you all for being here tonight to celebrate the launch of our first album," he said.

The guests cheered.

"None of this could have happened without the help of some very special people," Ollie continued. "To show our thanks, we've put together a little musical tribute . . . to the two ladies who've made all this possible."

A spotlight circled the dance floor and fell on Donna and Lark.

"We know we may not be the easiest houseguests to live with," said Max, stepping up to the mic. "But Donna and Lark, you didn't just open up your home to us, you opened your hearts as well. So, to our manager and our friend, this one's for you!"

With that, the boys launched into an a cappella version of a classic from the 1950s, "Donna," by Ritchie Valens. Despite the fact that the song was an oldie, Abbey Road had managed to modernize it in a way that had the crowd snapping their fingers along with the music.

"They're amazing," said Donna, tearing up yet again. "Maybe we *should* consider having them do some cover versions."

"As long as it isn't the Squirmies," Lark quipped.

Lark couldn't possibly imagine when they'd had time to learn and rehearse the song, but the fact that they had gone to such trouble made her heart swell with gratitude and affection.

When the performance was over, the guests exploded into applause and Donna headed onto the stage to accept hugs from the boys.

Ollie handed her the mic.

"Thank you, Abbey Road, for that wonderful tribute!" said Donna. "And thanks to everyone here tonight celebrating with us. Your support and belief means so much. I'm happy to tell you, the album is selling like hot cakes! Although, since two-thirds of the band is British, maybe I should say it's selling like a full English breakfast."

Ollie and Max broke into laughter, as did Max's parents and his sister, Anna. Lark wasn't sure why the joke was funny, but she didn't care. She was filled with such a feeling of joy that she laughed, too.

"This is Abbey Road's big night," Donna went on, "and I'm sure it will be the first of many. But while I've got your attention, I have a surprise announcement to make. Then I'll let you all get back to the dancing."

"And the eating," said Ollie, earning a chuckle from the partygoers.

Donna took a deep breath and clasped her hands to her heart. "I am so very proud to tell you that Lotus Records has just entered into a development deal with one of music's brightest and most talented young artists."

Lark's eyes went wide. *No, Mom*, she willed silently. *Please don't.*

"An artist who already holds a very special place in my heart." Donna's eyes sparkled. "I have incredibly high hopes for her, not only as a songwriter, but as a performer as well. And her name is . . ."

Lark held her breath; she felt the blood drain from her face. She wasn't ready for this news to be made public yet— she was still getting used to it herself. And besides, this wasn't how she wanted Max, Ollie, and Teddy to find out about her decision. She wanted to share this news with them privately, not in the middle of their special night.

"Her name is . . ." Donna shaded her eyes from the

spotlight, just as Holly had done at the Opry, and found Lark in the crowd. She paused, taking in Lark's horrified expression. ". . . going to remain a secret for just a little bit longer."

The crowd let out a collective grumble of disappointment.

Donna recovered with a laugh. "And that is what we in the music business call creating a buzz! You'll know soon enough who Lotus's next big star is going to be. But tonight is all about these three talented boys and their dazzlingly successful future."

She nodded to DJ Lucious and the sound of Abbey Road's "Promises to Keep" filled the club.

Lark closed her eyes in relief. She could breathe again.

✳

The party went on for hours. The music was amazing, the dancing was a blast, and, despite Fitzy's harsh critique, the food was scrumptious.

But by midnight, Lark was feeling like she needed a breather.

She spotted Teddy leaning against the bar, sipping the night's signature drink—fresh-squeezed lemonade and a splash of pomegranate juice with frozen raspberries floating in the glass like ice cubes. Donna had christened the drink the "Moliveddy," by cleverly mashing the boys' three names together.

"Hey, Teddy, I was just going to step outside for a breath of fresh air," she said, accepting the frosty Moliveddy the bartender offered her. "Want to come with?"

Teddy looked at her like a drowning boy who'd just been thrown a lifeline. "Absolutely," he said. "I hear this place has a rooftop terrace."

As they made their way through the crowd, Lark noticed cameras going off everywhere. She squinted into the flickering glare. "Who let the vultures in?"

"Julia did," Teddy explained. "She handpicked the ones she thought could be trusted and invited them in. Said it would be great to have some candid photos of the party show up on the entertainment websites and in celebrity magazines."

"I hope she chose carefully," Lark muttered as the sound of shutters clicking followed them across the dance floor. "I've heard some real horror stories about the paparazzi."

Click.

Click.

Click.

FLASH!

Dodging a few more photographers, they asked a waitress where the stairs to the roof were located and headed up to the top floor. Stepping into the cool night air, Lark shivered.

"Cold?" asked Teddy.

"A little."

He slipped off his blazer and draped it over her shoulders. Lark smiled, knowing her daddy would consider this gesture very gentlemanly.

The terrace was empty, which was fine with Lark; even though she'd come a long way in getting over her shyness, she found all those loud voices and unfamiliar faces downstairs a little overwhelming. Right now, all she wanted was some tranquility, mixed with starlight.

They found a spot along the railing and gazed out over the lights of LA.

"So," Teddy began, swirling the raspberries in his glass, "I'm going to go out on a limb and guess that *you* are the bright young artist your mom made the announcement about."

"I am," admitted Lark. "I decided I wanted to give the music business a shot when I was in Nashville. I meant to tell you when I got home, but with all the excitement about the album and the party planning, I just never had the chance."

"Well, congratulations. That's huge." He gave her a smile that didn't quite reach his eyes.

"You seem kind of bummed," Lark observed. "What's wrong?"

"If I told you, you'd think I was the world's biggest jerk."

Lark had to stop herself from telling him she could never think of him as anything but the sweetest, coolest, cutest boy she knew. Instead she said, "I won't think that. I promise. You can tell me."

Teddy sighed. "Okay, well, as awesome as this night has been, to be honest, I kind of wish that the album wasn't such a huge hit."

Lark must have looked stunned by this admission, because Teddy hurried on.

"Not that I wanted it to crash and burn or be some epic fail or anything like that. I mean, of course I wanted it to be a hit . . . eventually. Just not *yet*. I guess I was hoping it would take a while for it to climb the charts."

"So you could take your time getting used to it," Lark finished for him. "Right?"

"Exactly. Everybody in the whole world dreams of overnight fame, and here's me, hoping for the opposite. Crazy, huh?"

Lark shook her head. "Not at all. I totally get what you mean. I feel the same way."

"You do?" Teddy smiled and this time it lit up his whole face. "I guess that's just one more thing we have in common."

Lark thought she might melt. "I guess it is," she agreed. "I'm all for taking this whole stardom thing slowly. That's why I only agreed to an artist development deal. I didn't want things to happen too fast."

Teddy looked out over the city, trying to make sense of things. "I guess I'm just scared that I'll never be normal again. What if I never get to hang out with my friends, or go fishing with my dad? What if this leave of absence turns out to be permanent and I never go back to school?"

Lark felt another chill. It seemed colossally unfair that Teddy would be leaving right when they were getting to know each other. She couldn't imagine what school would be like without him, which was odd since a few short months ago they'd never uttered so much as a word to each other.

"What do your parents think?" she asked.

"They're torn. They know this is the opportunity of a lifetime and they don't want me to miss it. I don't either. I mean, I'm sure it will be fun. And the money I earn is going right into my college fund. I like that I'll be able to pay my own tuition someday. It's just that there are a lot of trade-offs, you know?"

Lark nodded. Moving from Nashville to LA had been a major trade-off. She understood that sometimes you had to give up one thing to have another.

"On the upside," said Teddy, "the tutor who's coming on the road with us is an Ivy League genius. So I'm hoping he'll be able to catch me up on all the schoolwork I've been struggling with."

"Right," said Lark, trying to be cheerful despite the sadness that was coursing through her. "And look at it this way. You'll never have to eat in the cafeteria again. No more disgusting turkey-surprise casseroles."

"Definitely a plus," Teddy agreed with a grin.

"And you won't have to sit through another of Principal Hardy's assembly lectures on the evils of tardiness, or about how a tidy locker is a happy locker."

"True," said Teddy, brightening a bit. "And don't forget, no more crab soccer in gym class."

"Right," said Lark, laughing. "I know you won't miss that!"

"I won't," said Teddy. "But there is something I will miss. A lot."

Lark was surprised that her next words came out in a whisper: "What's that?" she asked.

"You," he whispered back. Then, with the silver moon shining above, Teddy Reese leaned in and pressed a kiss as soft as starlight to her cheek. "What I'll miss most of all is you."

CHAPTER FIFTEEN

Lark awoke late on Sunday morning with Teddy's kiss still tingling on her cheek. In a daze, she stepped into her slippers, threw on her robe, and dropped her phone into its pocket. Then, with a dreamy smile on her face, she practically floated downstairs.

Ollie and her mom were already at the kitchen table. She deduced that Max must be at the hotel where, compliments of Lark's songwriting earnings, he'd spent the night with his family.

As she padded across the breakfast nook, Ollie and Donna just stared at her, speechless. Her first thought was that the mascara she'd worn the night before had smudged all over her eyes and left her looking like a rabid raccoon. But a quick glance at her reflection in the stainless-steel milk pitcher told her that wasn't the case.

"What's wrong?" she asked, sliding into a chair.

"So . . . you haven't been online yet?" Ollie ventured cautiously.

"Nope. I just woke up." She reached for a muffin from the basket Fitzy had set in the center of the table. "Why? What's happening online?"

Donna and Ollie exchanged glances. Then, with a heavy sigh, Donna slid her laptop across the table for Lark to see the celebrity-gossip website on-screen.

"Pictures from the party?" Lark asked. "Cool. I guess Julia was right to let some of the paparazzi in." She smiled, popping a piece of muffin into her mouth as she admired a shot of the boys singing their tribute medley. "This is great publicity."

"Scroll down, love," said Ollie, his tone ominous.

Lark took another bite of the muffin and grazed her fingers over the track pad. "Hey, that's a great one of you and Jas, Ollie. And look, there's Max with his parents, and there's—" She broke off, nearly choking on the unchewed bite of muffin.

There on the screen was a shot of Teddy and Lark.

On the roof.

Under the stars.

With his hand lingering gently on her waist . . . and his lips pressed softly to her cheek!

*

"Oh. My. God! Ohmygod-ohmygod-ohmyGOD! No! Tell me this isn't happening!"

"Lark, calm down," said Donna, patting her arm. "Please. Relax."

"Relax? How can I relax? Did you see this?"

"Oh, we saw it," Ollie muttered, sipping his tea.

"I don't understand how this picture even got taken," Lark wailed, "let alone posted! There was no one else on that roof. We were alone."

"Which is a conversation we'll definitely be having at a later date," said Donna sternly. "Honestly, Lark, did you really think I'd be okay with you going up to the rooftop alone with a boy?"

"Mother!" shrieked Lark, glaring at Donna. "That is so not the issue right now."

"I'm sorry, you're right." Donna looked instantly contrite. "I guess there was a photographer hiding up there somewhere. He must have taken the photo with some kind of high-powered zoom lens."

Lark's eyes shot back to the screen. "Can we make them take it down?" Her voice quivered on the cusp of hysteria as she frantically pounded the computer keys, desperate to make the photo disappear. "Can you sue somebody, Mama? Can we delete it?"

Ollie shook his head. "Sorry, Lark. It's there to stay."

Lark stared at the photo. The irony was that it was an absolutely gorgeous picture—soft lighting, flattering angle, Teddy's hair falling just so, and just the tiniest hint of a surprised smile on Lark's face. She would have thought it was the best picture ever taken, her favorite photo of all time . . . if only it hadn't been *posted online*!

She was so engrossed in the image that it took her a moment to notice the headline looming over it in big block letters.

ABBEY ROAD'S KEYBOARD CUTIE COZIES UP TO THE BOSS'S DAUGHTER

Lark felt queasy, but forced herself to move on to the article beneath the photo. To her horror, she was mentioned in it by name. Even worse, there were already hundreds of comments from readers. None of them were happy with Lark. Several of them begged her to leave Teddy alone because "he belongs to his fans" and because "U R not good enough for him!"

To Lark's horror, some of the insults had been hashtagged—and were trending:

#ScrawnyRedHead

#WastedKisses

#TweenTease

#PastYourBedtime

More than a few joked that the kiss had to be a publicity stunt, since an up-and-coming star like Teddy Reese could have any girl in the world, so why would he settle for a middle-school nobody like her?

Lark didn't know how long she'd been staring at the laptop when she felt Ollie reach across the table to gently slide it away.

And it wasn't until she saw the tears puddling on her breakfast plate that she realized she was crying.

✻

Lark set her phone on Do Not Disturb and spent the rest of the day and night in bed, huddled under the covers.

She thought about texting Teddy, but decided against it. She had absolutely no idea what to say to him, and she was sure he was feeling as embarrassed as she was, maybe even more. What kind of messages was *he* getting? She was afraid to even imagine.

On Monday morning, she considered skipping school.

Then she entertained the notion of dropping out altogether.

And then she got out of bed, got dressed, and marched

to the bus stop. Because deep down Lark knew that if this was a country song about a girl's first kiss getting hijacked by the media, the girl in question would not go down without a fight! She'd pull on her boots, muster up some Southern sass, and jerk a knot in somebody's tail!

Too bad there isn't a song like that, Lark thought.

And then, suddenly . . . there was. Her emotions were so pumped up that the lyrics came into her head like a hurricane. The song formed so quickly, she didn't even have time to pull her journal out of her backpack and write the words down:

> *Caught on camera, private touch.*
> *Picture perfect? Not so much!*
> *Somebody launched a sneak attack*
> *But it's my moment, so give it back!*
> *You can't get away with this,*
> *Go on and give me back my kiss!*

✳

From the minute she entered the school building, Lark was the recipient of a lot of dirty looks—from the girls who had major crushes on Teddy the pop star, and also from the ones who'd probably liked him long before he became part of the band. Just like Lark herself had.

The seventh and eighth graders muttered and sneered. The sixth graders mostly giggled and pointed. Lark heard the word "kiss" whispered and hissed behind her back so much that she felt as if she were being followed around by a giant snake.

By the time she reached her homeroom, she almost wished she'd stayed home. If only she could go back and erase all the publicity! But as her father would say, "the horse was already outta the barn." The damage was done and she had no choice but to face it.

The only upside (which, of course, was also a downside) was the fact that Teddy wasn't there. The announcement of the imminent tour had prompted his parents to take him out of school immediately. He was probably sitting down with his brand-new tutor at that very moment, catching up on science terminology and mathematical properties.

Somehow, Lark managed to get through homeroom and her first four classes without dying of embarrassment. Then she hunkered down in a far corner of the library during lunch to avoid the widespread exposure (not to mention the turkey-surprise casserole). The worst part was that she had yet to talk to Mimi about any of it.

Lark would have called her, but she simply couldn't bring herself to even *look* at her phone, for fear of seeing more nasty comments online. The last comment she'd read had been last night, just before she fell asleep, and it had forced her to power down her phone completely:

#Teddy'sGirlFIEND.

At first she mistook it for a compliment with an unfortunate typo, but she soon realized that the absence of the *R* was no accident. She'd been called a *fiend* ... as in a demon! The fact that it was overly dramatic and ridiculous didn't make it any less hurtful.

Unfortunately, Lark's self-imposed phone fast had resulted in zero communication with Mimi. And if ever there was a time she needed to talk to her best friend, this was it.

Finally, the part of the day she'd been dreading most arrived: sixth-period history. The only class besides gym that she had with Alessandra Drake.

Luckily, Mimi was also in that class.

Lark entered the classroom, murmured hello to Mr. Corbin, and took her seat. Mimi came in one minute later.

But she didn't even spare Lark a glance.

Lark's heart sank. *Uh-oh. This isn't good.*

Ally Drake wasted no time. "Nice kiss," she said in her snarkiest tone. "I'm not sure if you realize it, but kisses usually take place on the lips."

"It wasn't that kind of kiss," said Lark through her teeth.

"Well *obviously*. Anyway, I'm sure Teddy wasn't kissing you because he wanted to."

"Why else would he kiss her?" Jessica piped up, although Lark suspected it was more out of curiosity than any desire to defend Teddy's romantic impulse.

193

"Duh!" Ally tossed her hair and began ticking off the reasons on her fingers. "One, he's the new kid in the band; two, he's not British; and three, he's younger than the other two." She snickered. "Clearly, he wanted to stand out and make an impression on the boss."

"The boss?" Duncan echoed.

"Lark's mom. She hired Teddy, so she can fire him." Ally gave Lark a cold look. "But Teddy knows that no mom would ever fire her daughter's boyfriend."

"So you're saying Teddy kissed Lark just to suck up to Mrs. Campbell and get on her good side?" Jessica concluded.

"Well, it's either that or the boy just can't resist skinny girls in ugly boots." Ally gave a sarcastic roll of her eyes. "My money's on the sucking up."

During all of this, Lark had been gripping her pencil so tightly she was surprised it didn't shatter into a million yellow splinters. Every muscle in her body had gone tense and she was sure her face was redder than the stripes on Mr. Corbin's authentic Revolutionary War–era American flag.

She could have told Ally to leave her alone.

She could have told her she didn't know what she was talking about and was just jealous that Lark had gone to such a cool music-industry bash.

She could have, but she didn't.

Because she was waiting for Mimi to do it.

But for the first time since Lark had known her, her quick-thinking, outspoken best friend didn't appear to have anything to say.

And for Lark, Mimi's silence was way more heartbreaking than anything Alessandra Drake could have ever said out loud.

✳

When the bell rang and the rest of the class scrambled out of their seats, Lark hung back.

"Mimi, wait."

Mimi looked up from angrily stuffing her history textbook into her backpack. "Why? Do you have something to *tell* me?"

Lark almost laughed. "You must be kidding. I have like a *million* things to tell you! Starting with—"

"Forget it," Mimi interrupted with a snort. "I don't even care."

"What? Meems!"

"Anything you tell me now is old news," Mimi said stiffly.

"What are you talking about?"

Mimi shrugged. "You want to tell me how you wore your hair to the party? Too late—I already saw an in-depth analysis on Seventeen.com. Or maybe you want to tell me about how you danced with Max and then you and your mom got serenaded by the band? Sorry, already saw the video on E! Online. Hmmm, how about the mystery artist who's signing a development deal with Lotus? Don't bother, *Entertainment Tonight* covered that on their Sunday edition. I'm not stupid; I know the mystery artist is you!"

She let out a phony gasp of excitement. "Oh, I know! I bet you want to tell me all about how Teddy Reese, who as far as I knew was 'just a friend,' kissed you on a secluded rooftop terrace under the stars? Well, save your breath, Campbell, because I already know all about it. Just like everybody else on the planet!"

Lark felt as if she'd been slapped. "Mimi, I don't understand why you're so upset!"

Mimi's eyes flashed. "I'm *upset* because you and I are supposed to be best friends, which means that I should have known about that kiss before anyone! Before Perez Hilton and TMZ, and definitely before Ally Drake! You promised I'd be the first to know if anything changed between you and Teddy, but suddenly it seems like your life is going in a whole new direction and I'm the last person to hear about it."

Lark shook her head. "It wasn't like that! I wasn't trying to keep any of it from you! It's just, with the party, and the kiss, and then all those nasty comments online, I never got the chance to call you. I couldn't find the time."

"So that's how it is?" Mimi jerked her backpack onto her shoulder and scowled. "You're just *sooooo* busy with your boy-band boyfriend, and your cowboy music career, that you *can't find time* for me?!"

"No . . . !"

"Just because you're going to be famous and hang out with pop stars, you think you're better than boring old middle-school Mimi Solis."

"I didn't say that!"

"You didn't have to." Mimi narrowed her eyes.

"Mimi, please let me explain . . ."

"I would, but that might take a while, and I'm sure you've already wasted enough of your precious *time* on me. You probably have big plans with your teen-idol boyfriend."

"I told you!" shouted Lark. "Teddy is *not* my boyfriend!"

"Tell that to the Hollywood Reporter!" Mimi snapped, then turned and stormed out of the room.

CHAPTER
SIXTEEN

Every concert venue in America, it seemed, wanted Abbey Road on their schedule, so requests for dates and engagements continued to roll in. New York, Chicago, Kansas City, Denver . . .

Lark tried not to dwell on the fact that these additional concerts would only make the band's tour last longer. Instead of the three months they had originally booked, the extra dates had extended the tour to four months, pushing their time on the road well into June. Which meant Teddy would not get to finish out the school year.

Somehow, her schoolmates had convinced themselves that Teddy's leaving RRMS was entirely her fault. It was hard to shake off the fact that everyone at school was basically giving her the cold shoulder. But worst of all, Mimi still hadn't forgiven her.

Since Abbey Road would be performing a two-hour concert complete with a light show and dance numbers, Lark's former music room no longer cut it as a suitable practice area. So Donna rented a real rehearsal space in the downtown area where the boys could prepare for the tour. Consequently, they were hardly ever at home, which was terribly disappointing to Lark. She had hoped to spend as much time as possible with them before they left.

Finally, the Sunday afternoon of the band's departure was upon them. Just after lunch, a humongous tour bus came chugging up the Campbells' drive like some kind of motorized mythical creature.

Max and Ollie bounded out of the house and boarded the bus almost before the driver had cut the ignition. Standing in the driveway, Lark and Donna could hear them hooting and hollering about how awesome it was inside.

"We'll be like the Rolling Stones!" said Ollie. "Only younger."

"I prefer to think of myself as a young Lenny Kravitz," Max countered. "That dude's got style!"

When the boys came galloping out, it was Donna and Lark's turn to investigate the vehicle's interior.

"Pretty swanky, huh?" said Donna, eyeing the leather upholstery and shiny wood-veneer walls.

Lark wasn't sure she'd describe it quite that way. To her, it mostly seemed cramped and dark. It did, however, have plenty of cool amenities. There were four built-in bunks with curtains for privacy. There was a very tiny lavatory, a miniature galley kitchen, and loads of electronics. Everything seemed to be operated by push buttons. There was no denying that this was one upscale ride, but in truth, when Lark looked at it, all she could see was that the boys would be rolling out of her life for the foreseeable future.

When Lark exited the bus, she nearly crashed into Teddy, who was standing in the driveway with his suitcases, staring up at the behemoth that was about to become his home for the next four months.

It was the first time Lark had been in his company since the night of the Abbey Road party.

Since the night of their kiss.

"Hi." She smiled.

"Hi." He smiled back.

Lark noted silently that these were probably the two most awkward smiles ever exchanged in the history of the universe.

"My parents just dropped me off," Teddy explained. "My mom was pretty emotional, so they didn't stick around. Long good-byes, you know . . ."

Lark nodded.

"So. How've you been?"

"All right. How about you?"

Teddy shrugged. "Not bad. So, um . . . about that . . . you know . . ."

"Yeah." Lark kicked at a pebble on the asphalt. "I know. I'm sorry if it made things weird."

"What? No. I'm the one who should be sorry. I'm the one who gave you the . . . you know."

Lark grinned in spite of herself. "The kiss? It's okay, Teddy. You can say it."

"Okay. The kiss. I'm sorry I kissed you. I mean, I'm not sorry that I . . . I'm just . . ." He let out a long flustered breath and shook his head. "I'm sorry about all that stuff on the Internet."

"It's not your fault things got out of hand like they did. You didn't know there was a photographer hiding on the roof terrace."

"You're right. I didn't." Teddy looked overwhelmingly relieved. "And I'm really glad you feel that way. I was worried you were mad."

"Oh, *I'm* not mad," Lark assured him. "But your fans are a whole other story."

Teddy blushed. Then he laughed.

Lark laughed too.

The awkwardness was quickly fading away, and suddenly she was happy just to be talking to him again. "Excited for the tour?"

"Excited. And a little scared."

"That sounds about right."

"How about you? Are you looking forward to having the house to yourself?"

"Not as much as you might think," Lark admitted. "I've gotten used to having Max and Ollie around, even if they do sometimes drive me crazy."

"Well, I guess for the next few months they'll be driving me crazy," Teddy observed. "If you want, I'll take notes and send you updates, so you won't feel left out of all the craziness."

Lark managed to smile at that, but inside she felt a tug at her heart. Ordinarily, she'd be memorizing every word of this interaction with Teddy so that she could share it with Mimi and they could analyze the exchange—but that wasn't going to happen this time. Because Mimi still wasn't talking to her.

The next thing Lark knew, Oliver and Max were thundering out of the house with duffel bags slung over their shoulders. Ollie was toting his beloved Stratocaster and Max had his drumsticks in one hand and an electronic keyboard tucked under his arm.

"There he is," said Ollie, by way of a greeting. "So what do you think of our new home?"

"I've only seen the outside," Teddy told him. "Is it roomy?"

"Hah!" said Max with a big grin. "Let's put it this way . . . I really hope you don't snore."

"I don't," Teddy promised.

Ollie turned to Lark and gently chucked her under the chin. "All right, then. I guess this is good-bye for now. We'll miss you."

Lark felt a lump well up in her throat. "I'll miss you, too."

When Max gave her a hug, Lark's first thought was, *Please don't let there be a photographer in the bushes!* Her second thought was that the brotherly embrace was one of the sweetest things she'd ever felt.

"Keep in touch," he said softly. "Call us anytime."

"Same goes for you," said Lark. "I want to hear everything."

Ollie laughed. "Maybe not *everything*," he said, winking. "Just the PG stuff."

"There's only going to *be* PG stuff," Donna said sternly, appearing from the house. She was wheeling a designer suitcase and looked every inch the successful record-label boss. "Abbey Road is all about being wholesome and well-behaved, remember?"

"Of course we remember," teased Max. "You won't let us forget!"

"Just doing my job," said Donna.

Then a wave and a nod from the driver told them it was time to go.

Lark was overcome by such sadness that her knees nearly buckled. They weren't even on the bus yet and already she felt indescribably lonely.

Fitzy came rushing through the front door, weeping

profusely and carrying a stack of Tupperware containers, which she handed to the bus driver. "I've packed you some snacks," she announced. "Parsnip scones, mango-chunk oatmeal cookies, and Tex-Mex meatloaf with wasabi sauce!"

Max laughed. "Your greatest hits!"

"What?" cried Ollie, giving her a loud smooch on the cheek. "No Yorkshire pudding?"

"Oh, you!" Fitzy swatted him away, then burst into a fresh shower of tears and hurried back into the house.

"All right," said Donna. "All aboard!"

"I call top bunk," said Ollie, racing toward the bus.

"I call other top bunk," said Max, hot on his heels.

Lark laughed and gave Teddy a sympathetic smile. "Good luck!"

"Thanks." Teddy took two steps toward the bus, then turned back, gave her a wave, and disappeared into the belly of the bus-beast.

"Well," said Donna.

"Well," said Lark.

"I'll only be gone for a week," Donna reminded her. "I just want to get the boys settled and make sure the first few concerts go smoothly. Then I'll be home and I'll only be flying out from time to time to check on them." She smiled. "After all, Lotus has a new talent in development, and it's high time I gave her my undivided attention. Now come over here, darling, and give your mama a hug!"

Lark did. The only good thing about this tour was that, in addition to the Ivy League tutor, Donna was sending Julia the PR girl and a handful of other responsible professionals along to keep an eye on the boys and handle their business concerns. Lark would have hated it if her mom had deemed it necessary to join the boys for the entire time they'd be on the road.

She watched as Donna loaded her fancy suitcase into the cargo hold and hurried up the bus steps. Then the engine growled, the driver honked the horn, and the enormous machine backed out to the street.

Lark watched it go, leaving her in the driveway all alone. She walked slowly into the house. With any luck, she'd find some of her favorite kind of company . . . the company of a song.

✳

Okay, so maybe it wasn't *exactly* like getting out of the limo in front of Dusk.

There were no velvet ropes, no pale-blue lighting, no line of elegant party guests, and no huddle of eager paparazzi awaiting the arrival of entertainment's newest stars.

Today there were just giggling students and lunch trays and rolling trash barrels.

But what *was* the same was the way everyone stared when Lark appeared in the caf-a-gym-a-torium doorway. Heads began to turn, one by one at first, then table by table. Kids pointed and whispered as Lark strode toward the table by the window where Mimi was seated alone, hunched over an uninspiring sloppy joe, oblivious to the strange scene that was unfolding thanks to the earbuds she was wearing.

Lark pushed aside the nervous feeling that tingled in her belly. She ignored the nosy looks and curious murmurs. She even managed to disregard Ally Drake, who said loudly in her most condescending tone, "*What* is she carrying in that big, ugly case?"

Lark let Ally's question go unanswered and kept right on walking.

Because Lark was on a *mission*.

And the mission was music.

Mimi looked up from her lunch with a start when Lark slid the guitar case across the lunch table. "What's going on?" she asked, jerking the headphones out of her ears.

"I guess you could call it a world premiere," said Lark, lovingly removing the old Gibson from its battered case. Slipping the strap over her head, she arranged her fingers on the strings.

Mimi's eyes were round with astonishment.

"I apologize if I'm a little shaky," Lark said with a shrug. "I still haven't completely kicked the whole stage-fright thing. But the funny thing is, once a girl plays the Grand

Ole Opry, the Ronald Reagan Middle School caf-a-gym-a-torium doesn't seem all that scary anymore. And besides, some things are worth being scared for."

She closed her eyes and swept her fingers over the strings. Images of herself and Mimi laughing by the pool, watching music videos, and even choking down Fitzy's not-so-famous mustard donuts filled her mind like scenes from a favorite movie while her voice filled the lunchroom.

I don't say it often, because I thought you knew,
How much you mean to me, and the way I feel 'bout you.
So now, my friend, I want to make you see,
How much your friendship means to me . . .

Out of the corner of her eye, Lark spotted the lunch-duty teacher, a frowning Coach Bricker, preparing to storm across the caf-a-gym-a-torium. But as luck would have it, Principal Hardy, who was just exiting the lunch line with a chef's salad and diet iced tea, stopped him with a smile and an authoritative shake of her head.

They say that time is precious and I don't disagree,
Because the time I spend with you means so much to me.
And one thing's for certain, on this you can depend:
There'll always be time for me to be your friend.

The final note trembled away, settling into the silence that had fallen over the lunchroom.

A silence that didn't last long.

In the next heartbeat, everyone (even Coach Bricker) was applauding and cheering for Lark's performance.

Everyone except Mimi.

Because Mimi was too busy hugging Lark.

"Best friends?" Lark whispered into Mimi's ear.

"Best *best* friends," Mimi replied.

Lark smiled. Mission (and music) accomplished!

CHAPTER SEVENTEEN

"Will you please pass the sunscreen?" Lark's voice was a lazy singsong that caught itself in a warm spring breeze. It was Friday, and school had let out early for a teacher's workshop, giving the girls the whole luxurious afternoon to lounge by the pool.

Mimi obliged, tossing a bottle of SPF 50 onto Lark's lounge chair.

A couple months had passed since the boys had left on their tour. Lark still missed them terribly, but the fact that school was winding down and summer vacation was right around the corner made it a little easier to take.

Donna had flown out three days earlier to meet the boys in Las Vegas, to check up on things and discuss plans for the second album. She'd be riding the bus with them back to California for a show that weekend.

"Thanks, Meems," said Lark, rubbing the sunscreen onto her cheeks.

"No probs. I can't have the star of my next music video getting sunburned."

"I told you, the song isn't ready yet. And besides, don't you have enough to do as the Lotus Records media intern?"

"You know that's all on hold until the boys get back from tour." Mimi sighed. "Although it would have been awesome if I could have tagged along and shot some live concert footage."

"Speaking of the tour, is there anything about it online today?"

"That's a silly question," said Mimi, grabbing her iPad from the little glass table between their chairs. "Since there's been something about Abbey Road on the entertainment sites every single day since the tour began."

Lark grinned, her eyes crinkling behind her aviator sunglasses. "Mom is thrilled about that, since all the reviews and articles have been so positive."

"Okay, let's see . . ." Mimi scrolled through the recent news on the tablet. "This music critic from *Rolling Stone* calls them 'worthy of their Beatles-inspired name.' And *People* can't say enough about how charming and clean-cut they are." She read silently for a bit, then giggled. "This journalist calls Ollie 'a natural-born superstar.' And he says Max is too talented to pin down—he can't decide whether to refer to him as the drummer or the dancer, so he's coined a new term: 'the drancer.' "

"Does it say anything about Teddy?" Lark asked.

"Yep. Says he's a gifted musician, a charismatic performer, and most of all . . . 'one of the most adorable teen idols America has ever seen.' " Mimi looked up from the tablet and smiled. "Must be nice to hear someone say that stuff about your boyfriend."

"Mimi, he's *not* my boyfriend!" *At least, I don't think he is.*

Mimi rolled her eyes. "Well, I wish he were!"

"Why would *you* wish it?"

"Because if he were your boyfriend, you'd have already finished writing the song, and we'd be working on our next video. I mean, it's pretty obvious from the lyrics you've shown me so far that the song is about him. Isn't it?"

Lark chose not to comment. Mimi was right, of course. Her latest work in progress was all about her feelings for Teddy. Unfortunately, the primary feeling in the mix was confusion. Sure, he'd kissed her on the cheek in the moonlight, but that was a while ago at this point. Other than their one clunky conversation in the driveway, they hadn't really had a chance to talk about it. She had no idea what he was thinking or feeling.

"Have you heard from him?" Mimi persisted.

"Yeah, he's texted a few times, but it's mostly just small talk and concert updates. Like, 'Max lost his drumsticks in

Atlanta,' and 'Ollie forgot the words to "Wounded Pride" in Phoenix.' "

"So nothing juicy and meaningful like, 'Lark, I'm counting the minutes until I can gaze into your beautiful green eyes again'?"

"Nope." Lark gave a long sigh. "Nothing like that."

"Well," said Mimi, her fingers fluttering over the tablet screen, "if it's any consolation, I'm looking at the band's Instagram account right now and there aren't any pictures of Teddy smooching or . . . what was that word Max taught you . . . swogging?"

"Snogging."

"Right, snogging. There is not one single photo of Teddy snogging any girls." Mimi laughed. "Although there *is* one of him getting licked by a golden retriever puppy."

"Well, now I'm *really* jealous!" joked Lark. "I love golden retriever puppies!"

Mimi laughed, then stood up, collected her towel and sunscreen, and stuffed them in her bag. "I've got to run. Why don't you go and work your musical magic on the Teddy song? It would be great if we could start filming next week."

"Fine," said Lark, rising from the chaise longue. "I'll see if I can bang out a few solid verses. But I'm not making you any promises. Magic takes time, you can't just make it happen."

"There you go!" cried Mimi, giving a little skip as she headed across the lawn. "That could be a lyric right there—

magic takes time! If that doesn't describe your relationship with Teddy Reese, I don't know what does!"

✳

When Lark wandered into the practice room, loneliness hit her like a punch. She'd have given anything to see Ollie sprawled on the carpet with a bowl of ice cream, or Max twirling his drumsticks between his fingers.

The room felt cold and empty.

Kind of like Lark, when she thought about Teddy, and whether or not his feelings for her were anything like her feelings for him.

Dropping into the armchair, she clicked her tongue for Dolly. The cat came slinking out from where she'd been sleeping under one of Ollie's sweaters, which had been left in a heap on the floor.

"You miss them too, huh, girl?" said Lark, drawing the graceful little cat into her lap.

Dolly replied with a purr, which Lark took to mean, *You bet I do.*

With Dolly settled back to sleep and her guitar across her legs, Lark opened her songwriting journal, closed her eyes, and waited for the magic to happen.

Musical notes appeared like snowflakes, spiraling through the darkness behind her eyelids. They found their way to her fingers, and she began to play.

The words followed soon enough, and two hours later, she was singing her new song to her father on the computer.

"So what do you think, Daddy?"

"I think it could be another hit for the Hatfields," Jackson said.

"Uh-uh." Lark shook her head. "This one's mine."

On the computer screen, Jackson frowned. "That's what I was afraid of."

"What do you mean?"

"It's just that those lyrics are . . ." Jackson paused to scratch his scruffy beard. "Well, they're a little more mature than your usual stuff."

Lark shrugged. "I guess. But it's how I feel. Is that wrong?"

"Not wrong at all, darlin'," said Jackson. "I just don't want you to grow up too fast is all. I mean, first the development deal, and now . . ." He sighed. "Now a full-on love song."

"Daddy!" Lark felt a prickle of embarrassment. "How can you say it's a love song when the word 'love' isn't even in it?"

Jackson chuckled. "It may not be in the lyrics, but it's definitely implied."

Lark considered this. "Okay, maybe it is, but that's how it is with songwriting. Sometimes you have to exaggerate for artistic purposes." She smiled. "I promise, Daddy, you have got nothing to worry about. Heck, just being 'in like' is confusing enough for me right now."

After they ended their video call, Lark joined Fitzy in the kitchen to help her make dinner—chicken stir-fry with basmati rice and a surprisingly tasty cheesecake with jalapeño compote for dessert. She did her homework and let Fitzy check her geography assignment. As it turned out, Fitzy's girlhood obsession with flying airplanes and traveling the globe had made her an expert at geography.

And then, Lark's phone rang.

Lark checked the caller ID, half hoping it would be Teddy. It wasn't.

"Hi, Mom."

"Hello, honey. Listen, I can't talk long, the boys are due at the concert venue in twenty minutes. I just wanted to ask you a couple of quick questions."

"Okay," said Lark. "Shoot."

"Question number one: Have you heard of Springsong, the annual music festival in Palm Springs?"

"Sure," said Lark. "It's super famous. It's a weekend-long concert. All the biggest acts take part, and it always gets sold out in, like, the first hour after tickets go on sale."

"That's right," said Donna.

"What's the second question?"

"How would you like to go?"

CHAPTER
EIGHTEEN

"I can't believe Abbey Road got a last-minute spot at Spring-song," said Lark when she and Fitzy hopped into the car early the next morning.

"And I can't believe I'm driving all the way to Palm Springs," Fitzy grumbled, backing Donna's SUV out of the driveway. "It's the first Saturday in May, the day I always do my mega spring cleaning. I've got windows to wash and floors to wax, and I was really hoping to regrout the tile in the guest bathroom this afternoon."

"Who wants to regrout a bathtub when they can go to the coolest concert of the year?" Lark protested.

"Me, that's who," said Fitzy with a sniff. "Now, open that Tupperware container. I packed us some tofu cannoli for the ride."

Once the world's most conscientious housekeeper had

gotten past her disappointment over not being able to spend the day beating rugs and polishing furniture, the mood in the SUV improved greatly. The drive to Palm Springs was just over two hours, and Lark and Fitzy spent it happily quizzing each other on music trivia. Lark was amazed to discover that Fitzy was an expert on classic rock and roll. Fitzy even rattled off a list of some of the more unusual jobs held by rock stars prior to their becoming famous: one had been a grave digger! Who knew?

When they reached the outdoor venue where Springsong was taking place, Fitzy pulled into the parking lot and flashed the VIP pass Donna had e-mailed. This allowed them to drive right up to the event area.

Lark gasped when she saw how many people were there—and it was only ten o'clock in the morning! Not surprisingly, the crowd was made up primarily of teenagers and college students.

"Should've brought my Frisbee," Fitzy quipped as they got out of the car. "Not to mention my hand sanitizer."

"There you are!" came a familiar voice.

"Mama!" Lark bolted across the dusty dirt parking lot and threw her arms around Donna.

"There's my girl!" Donna covered Lark's face with kisses.

"And where are those Abbey Road hooligans?" Fitzy asked.

"Why?" Donna teased. "Do you miss them?"

"Not at all," Fitzy lied with an airy wave of her hand.

Donna led them to where several tour buses were parked. Lark had no trouble picking Abbey Road's bus out of the group. She ran for it and bounded up the steps.

"Hey, y'all," she said.

"Lark!" cried Max, ruffling her hair as Ollie caught her in a rib-squashing hug.

But Teddy was nowhere to be seen.

"Don't look so glum," said Max with a chuckle. "Your boy just went to buy us some sodas. He'll be back in a minute."

When Fitzy and Donna joined them, Lark was afraid Fitzy might actually go into cardiac arrest over the condition of the bus. The countertops were piled high with dirty dishes and empty pizza boxes and the floor was strewn with filthy socks and damp towels.

"What are you boys?!" cried Fitzy, aghast. "Animals?"

"Worse," said Oliver. "We're pop stars."

Max laughed. "Sorry, Fitz. I guess we've gotten a little behind on our household chores."

As Fitzy gazed around at the mess, a smile spread across her face. "I guess I'm going to do my spring-cleaning after all," she said, rolling up her sleeves.

"Oh, Mrs. Fitzpatrick," said Donna. "You don't have to do that."

"Are you kidding?" cried Fitzy, eagerly gathering up the dirty T-shirts and blue jeans from the floor. "This is the kind of challenge I live for! And besides, unless Van Halen is planning to make a surprise appearance, I'd much rather be in here changing bed linens and cleaning out the fridge."

Max gave Fitzy a pout. "What about us? We go on at noon."

"I'll poke my head out to watch you perform, of course," she assured him. "God knows I'll need the fresh air! But other than that, I've got my work cut out for me. It's a wonder the health department hasn't had this bus condemned!"

Fitzy had a valid point. The stench of moldy half-eaten tacos and unwashed socks was beginning to make Lark a little queasy.

Leaving a giddy Fitzy behind to revel in her task, Lark, Donna, Ollie, and Max exited the bus, just as Teddy was returning with three frosty Cokes.

His eyes lit up when he saw Lark, and she had a sneaking suspicion hers did exactly the same. For a moment, the two of them just stood there, staring at each other with goofy grins on their faces.

When it became clear that Teddy had forgotten all about the drinks he was carrying, Max carefully removed the three bottles from his grasp.

"Hey, Max," said Ollie, "how about we go introduce ourselves to that blond singer from, er, Canada and congratulate her on her number-one single?"

"Sounds like a plan," said Max, taking the hint.

"Oh!" Donna chimed in. "And I . . . um . . . I really need to go and call the lawyers about . . . um . . . well, about some very important paperwork! You know how it is with paperwork."

Lark had no idea how it was with paperwork, and she was pretty sure there was no Canadian singer either. They were all just making excuses—and none too smoothly—to give her and Teddy a few minutes alone.

She wasn't sure whether she wanted to thank them or clobber them.

"How's touring?" asked Lark, at the exact moment that Teddy asked, "How's school?"

"Touring's tiring," answered Teddy, at the same time that Lark replied, "School's boring."

"Want to take a walk?" Teddy asked. "There're a lot of cool souvenir booths and food trucks and other stuff we can explore. We might even run into some of the big-name acts. I have to admit, I'm a little starstruck."

"I didn't know stars could get starstruck," Lark said. She was glad to discover that Teddy's newfound fame hadn't gone to his head.

As they wandered the grounds, Teddy got stopped once or twice by autograph seekers and fans wanting to take a selfie with him. Mostly, though, they went unnoticed, blending in with the youthful crowd.

The whole place was alive with sound and color and

energy. The band that was onstage was playing something bluesy, groups of friends were dancing and taking selfies, and Lark saw at least three couples making out. This made her blush, thinking back to that sweet rooftop moment with Teddy. She wondered if, after witnessing these bold public displays of affection, he would consider their kiss childish and silly.

In fact, she wondered if he thought *she* was silly. After all, he was a pop star about to perform at one of the most famous music festivals on the West Coast and she was still an ordinary middle-school girl.

She was just beginning to panic over the extended stretch of silence between them when Teddy turned to her and blurted out, "I really miss you."

Caught off guard, Lark blinked at him. "What?"

"I miss you," he repeated. "I hope you don't think this is weird of me to say, but I think about you a lot."

Lark smiled. "You do?"

"Yeah, I do. I miss hearing your thoughts on music, and talking to you about school. Before I left, I felt like we were really starting to connect, and I thought maybe you felt it, too."

Lark nodded. "I did."

"That's why I miss seeing you at school, and at your house during rehearsals," Teddy went on. "Being on tour is exciting, but other than Max and Ollie, it feels like the only people we ever see are grown-ups. The promoters, the roadies, our tutor—everybody's old. Not like ancient, but still, old."

"What about the fans?" asked Lark.

"We don't really interact with them much," Teddy explained. "And even when we do have a meet-and-greet or a photo op, the girls are all so . . . aggressive. They're either screaming or crying or grabbing at our clothes, or begging Ollie for his phone number. It's all kind of unreal. But, see, that's what I've always liked most about you, Lark. You're . . . *real*."

"Like a country song?" she said, grinning.

"Just like a country song."

It was the nicest thing he could have said to her. Emboldened by his honesty, she decided to do something honest too.

She reached out and took his hand.

"Look," she said. "I know this is a crazy time for you. But there's only one month left of the tour, and you're going to get through it, I promise. In the meantime, while you're out on the road, you can call me anytime you want. I'll always want to talk to you."

"Thanks. And I'll want to talk to you, too."

"And Donna wants to talk to *both* of you!" came a familiar and excited voice from behind them. "Now!"

Lark whirled to see Max approaching in a hurry.

"What's going on?" she asked. "Why does Mom want to talk to me?"

"Because she just spoke to the concert promoter," Max informed them. "Inner Truth, the band that was supposed to play right before us, is stuck somewhere out on Route 111. Their tour bus got a flat tire and they aren't going to make it here for at least another few hours."

"Wow, that stinks," said Teddy.

"Yeah," said Lark. "But what's it got to do with us?"

"The promoter needs to fill the spot," Max explained, beaming. "So Donna thought maybe Songbird might like to get her name on the bill."

CHAPTER NINETEEN

Lark's head was spinning.

They were back on the tour bus and she was seated on one of the freshly made bottom bunks, her feet tapping nervously inside her old boots.

"But I haven't rehearsed!" she protested.

"You don't need to rehearse," said Teddy. "You're a natural."

"And I don't have anything to wear!"

"The sundress you've got on is perfect," Donna assured her. "It will complement your country sound. They'll play you up as Lotus's newest star and introduce you as Songbird."

"Songbird, huh?" Lark gulped. If she did decide to go out onstage in front of all these people as Songbird, there would be no turning back—she would be revealed once and for all as the girl in the videos Mimi had posted online. Somewhere out there, GlitzyGirlFluffyFace would have a good laugh at Lark's expense.

So what? Who cares what someone called GlitzyGirlFluffy-Face thinks?

But still . . . YouTube was one thing; *this* was Springsong! All those cool people in the audience . . .

Then again, once a girl's played the Grand Ole Opry . . .

"What would I sing?" she heard herself asking. "I don't have my guitar."

"There are over nine hundred musicians performing at this festival," Donna said reasonably. "I'm pretty sure one of them would be kind enough to lend a guitar to a sweet young thing like you."

Okay, so it wouldn't be her Gibson, but she could work around that. Lark looked from Donna to Max, to Ollie and Fitzy, and finally to Teddy. "What do you think?"

"I think you'll knock 'em dead," said Max emphatically.

"Definitely," said Teddy.

"Go for it," said Ollie, giving her an encouraging little punch to the shoulder.

"Best opportunity ever," was Donna's professional opinion.

"Honey," said Fitzy, taking Lark's face in her hands and tilting it upward so their eyes met. "I never had my chance to fly. But today is your chance to soar."

There was a knock on the bus door and the promoter's assistant poked her head inside. "We're ready for"—she consulted her clipboard—"Songbird."

Lark's breath caught in her throat.

She looked around at the people she loved. She could feel their eyes on her, but more than that, she could feel their faith in her.

"All right," she said, pushing her shoulders back and lifting her chin. "You can tell them that Songbird's ready to sing."

*

Twenty minutes later, Lark took the stage to the sound of the announcer's voice. "Give it up for Lotus Records' hot new country sensation and YouTube star, Lark 'Songbird' Campbell."

The crowd offered only a tepid reception. After all, they'd been expecting Inner Truth, and here was a twelve-year-old girl in cowboy boots clutching a borrowed guitar.

Lark's gut instinct was to run.

But then she caught a glimpse of Abbey Road in the wings, urging her on with big smiles.

In that moment, she knew she couldn't fail.

She opened with "Everything's Working Out," then segued into "Homesick." Music spilled from her fingertips as her voice filled the desert air. Lark played two of Holly

Rose's current hits, then wowed the audience with the song she'd written in Nashville.

> *I'll make the rules and do it my way,*
> *Let me lead, or hit the highway.*
> *It's time to face the great unknown,*
> *But one thing's sure—I'll hold my own.*

When she finished, the crowd started chanting her name. "Song-bird! Song-bird! Song-bird!"

"Thank you so much," she said, her heart racing with joy. "I think I have time for one more before we bring on Abbey Road."

This inspired another eruption of cheers and applause.

"This is a song I just finished writing yesterday," she explained. "I wrote it about somebody who means the world to me. It's a song about those feelings of confusion everybody has once in a while. But I've got to tell you, today . . ." She darted a glance into the wings and met Teddy's gaze. "Well, today, I'm not feeling confused at all."

She took a deep breath and began to sing.

> *Do you remember when you kissed me?*
> *You're on the road, but do you miss me?*
> *I know your life is a crazy whirl,*
> *But all I want is to be your girl.*

The final note faded and the fans roared their approval.

"Thank you, Springsong!" Lark called out, waving both hands. "I hope you had as much fun as I did! I'm Songbird . . . and today is the day I learned to fly!"

The applause followed her as she ran off stage—where Teddy wrapped her in a hug.

"That one was for you," she whispered in his ear.

"I was hoping it was," he whispered back.

Then Max was tugging Teddy's sleeve and Abbey Road ran out onto the stage, to a maelstrom of shouts and cheers.

Breathless, Lark watched as Ollie positioned himself at the mic.

"Hello Palm Springs!" he cried, relishing the crowd's enthusiasm. "And . . . one, two, one two three four . . ."

When Abbey Road launched into the familiar lyrics of "Wounded Pride," thousands of fans sang along. It gave Lark goose bumps to hear all those voices singing words she'd written herself. She stood in the wings, feeling proud and amazed.

Songbird's first performance had happened on her own terms—her words, her music, her decisions. And although she had no idea what would come next in this brand-new music career of hers, she did know this much . . . it had definitely started on a high note!

And there was no better feeling in the world.